Echoes of the Missing

Echoes of the Missing

Cindy C

Published by Cindy C, 2024.

Copyright Page
Echoes of the Missing

This is a work of fiction. Similarities to real people, places, or events are entirely coincidental.

ECHOES OF THE MISSING

First edition. December 30, 2024.

Copyright © 2024 Cindy C.

ISBN: 979-8230121114

Written by Cindy C.

Table of Contents

Table of Contents

- A shocking discovery forces Sophia to confront unimaginable realities.

10. **Chapter Nine**

Echoes of the Missing

- The climactic confrontation where the pieces of the puzzle fall into place.

1. **Chapter Ten**

Shadows of Resolution

- Sophia must decide how far she is willing to go to protect her family and reveal the truth.

1. **Epilogue**

Lingering Whispers

- Reflections on the journey, the price of answers, and the echoes that remain.

Introduction

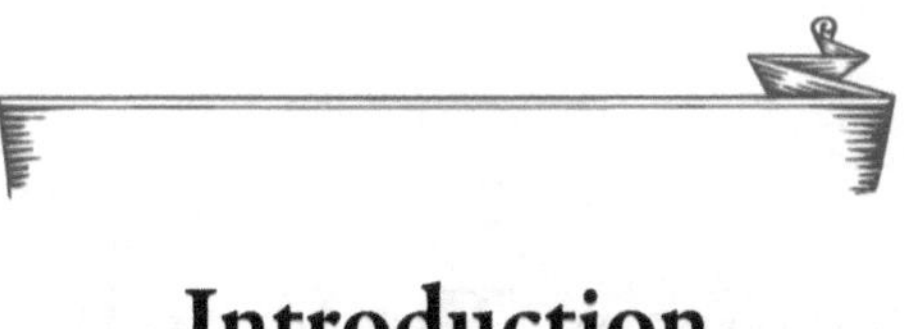

What if the people we've lost aren't entirely gone? What if echoes of their lives resonate in ways we can't fully comprehend?

Echoes of the Missing explores these questions through the journey of Sophia Reed, a mother whose life is turned upside down when her young daughter, Lily, begins to display knowledge of a life she never lived. As the lines between the past and the present blur, Sophia is drawn into a chilling mystery—a story of loss, identity, and the unbreakable bond between a mother and her child.

This is not just a tale of reincarnation or mystery. It's a story about the lengths we go to protect those we love, the courage to confront truths that defy logic, and the power of the human spirit to find meaning in the inexplicable.

Prepare yourself for a journey filled with suspense, emotional depth, and twists you won't see coming. Each page will pull you closer to the truth, challenging your perceptions of reality and the ties that bind us across time.

Welcome to *Echoes of the Missing*. The answers lie in the whispers of the past.

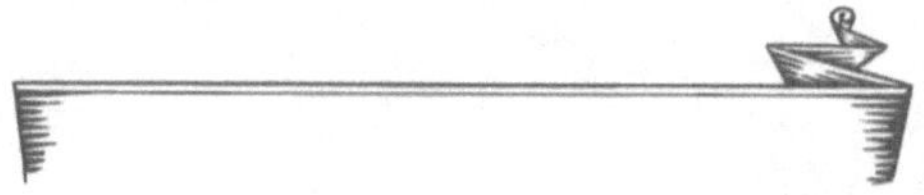

Prologue: The Vanishing

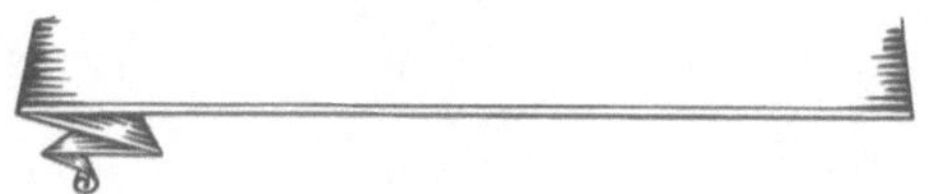

The night Clara Bennett disappeared was one of those peculiar evenings where the air seemed to hum with an unseen tension. It was late October, and the small town of Hartwell was cloaked in the sort of eerie silence that only deep autumn could bring. The streets, lined with skeletal trees, were empty save for the occasional rustle of dry leaves skittering across the cracked pavement. Clara's footsteps echoed softly as she walked along the dimly lit path leading to her house, a modest two-story structure perched at the edge of the woods.

Clara was a journalist, known for her relentless pursuit of the truth. In the months leading up to her disappearance, she had been working on an exposé about corruption in the highest levels of local government. Her colleagues whispered about threats she'd received, warning her to back off. But Clara was undeterred. She had always believed that the truth was worth any risk.

On this particular night, Clara clutched her worn leather satchel tightly against her side. Inside were notes, photographs, and an old USB drive—evidence she believed would blow the lid off her investigation. She felt a mix of fear and exhilaration as she turned onto the secluded dirt road that led to her home.

The events that followed would haunt Hartwell for years to come.

As Clara approached her house, a shadow moved just beyond the edge of the porch light. She froze, her breath catching in her throat. "Hello?" she called, her voice steady despite the thudding of her heart.

There was no response. The shadow vanished into the darkness as quickly as it had appeared.

Brushing it off as her imagination, Clara hurried up the steps and into the house, locking the door behind her. She placed her satchel on the kitchen table and poured herself a glass of wine, trying to calm her nerves. The house was unnervingly quiet, save for the rhythmic ticking of the grandfather clock in the hallway.

Then came the knock.

It was faint at first, so subtle she almost didn't hear it. But as she approached the front door, the knocking grew louder, more insistent. Through the peephole, she saw nothing but darkness. Her hand hovered over the deadbolt, a sense of dread creeping over her.

"Who's there?" she demanded. Silence.

Suddenly, the power went out. The house plunged into blackness, and Clara's pulse raced. Fumbling for her phone, she turned on the flashlight and backed away from the door. She was halfway to the kitchen when she heard it—a soft creak, the unmistakable sound of a floorboard shifting under weight. Someone was inside.

The next morning, Clara was gone.

Her house was eerily untouched, save for the broken lock on the back door. Her satchel, with all her evidence, was missing. The police found no signs of a struggle, no clues as to where she might have gone. It was as if she had simply vanished into thin air.

News of Clara's disappearance spread quickly through Hartwell, casting a shadow of fear and suspicion over the tight-knit community. Whispers of foul play grew louder, fueled by the knowledge of her dangerous investigation. Her family pleaded for answers, her colleagues rallied for justice, but as the weeks turned into months, hope began to wane.

Unbeknownst to the world, Clara Bennett's story was far from over. Her disappearance was not the end but the beginning of a mystery that would resurface years later in the most unexpected of ways—a mystery tied inexplicably to a young child's haunting recollections of a life she had never lived.

Chapter One: Unsettling Shadows

Sophia Reed was a woman of routine. Life as a single mother to her eight-year-old daughter, Lily, had taught her to embrace the predictable. Mornings consisted of rushed breakfasts, scattered school papers, and the comforting hum of the coffee maker. Evenings were spent finishing work, preparing dinner, and settling Lily into bed with a warm blanket and a bedtime story. But lately, something had started to disturb this peace—something Sophia could not explain, something that felt foreign in the very fabric of their home.

It began subtly. At first, Sophia didn't want to believe it was anything more than a phase. Children's imaginations were wild and unchecked, and at Lily's age, the line between reality and fantasy could often blur. But over the past few weeks, Lily's behavior had started to take on an unsettling quality, one that no longer seemed to be part of her normal whims.

It started one crisp autumn evening, as the sun dipped low on the horizon and the chill of the night began to creep through the cracks of their old house. Sophia was finishing up her work in the kitchen while Lily, as usual, was seated at the dining table, coloring in one of her many sketchbooks. The soft sound of her daughter's crayon against paper was the only noise filling the room, save for the ticking of the old clock on the mantle.

Sophia glanced over her shoulder, taking in the peaceful sight of Lily's small form hunched over her drawing. But then something struck her—a sense of quiet that felt too still, too eerie. Lily had been unusually silent, even for her.

Sophia walked over, leaning against the back of the chair where her daughter sat. "What are you drawing, honey?"

Lily didn't respond immediately. She looked at the page for a moment, as though lost in thought, and then slowly turned it toward her mother. The picture was unlike any other Sophia had seen.

It was a woman—a dark figure in the distance, blurred and shadowed, as though obscured by mist. The figure was standing on the edge of a cliff, looking out toward a vast, inky ocean, while strange, sharp rocks protruded from the ground around her. And though the figure was almost abstract, there was something disturbingly real about her—something that made Sophia's heart race with an unfamiliar dread.

Sophia blinked, momentarily taken aback by the haunting nature of the image. She could feel the hairs on the back of her neck rise. "Who is this, Lily?" she asked, her voice trembling slightly.

Lily looked up at her with wide eyes, her expression unreadable. "I don't know. I just... saw her, I guess."

Sophia forced a smile, trying to push the chill away. "You saw her? Where?"

Lily shrugged, her fingers tapping lightly on the edge of the table. "I don't know. I think I remember her... she was in a place... somewhere dark, somewhere cold. She wasn't looking at me, Mama. She was looking at something far away."

Sophia's heart beat faster, and for a moment, she couldn't find her voice. She felt a sudden, inexplicable panic rising in her chest. The image felt so familiar, so tangible, but she couldn't place where she had seen something like it before. She'd never seen anything like it in Lily's previous drawings.

"Sweetheart," Sophia said softly, her tone trying to steady herself, "are you sure you haven't seen this woman in a story or on TV?"

Lily shook her head. "No, Mama. I... I think she's waiting for someone. She's sad. She wants to go back, but she can't. She's lost."

Sophia's breath caught in her throat, and a cold shiver ran down her spine. The words were too heavy for a child her age. There was a depth to them that chilled her to the bone. As a mother, she wanted to comfort her daughter, reassure her that it was all just a figment of imagination. But in her gut, she knew something wasn't right.

The unease lingered in the back of Sophia's mind as she tucked Lily into bed that night. She kissed her forehead and whispered a soft "Goodnight, sweet girl," but as she stood at the door, she could still hear her daughter's soft muttering from the other side of the room.

"Mama," Lily's voice was a soft whisper, "I don't want to go back there. I don't want to see her again."

Sophia's hand froze on the door handle. "See who, honey?"

Lily didn't answer immediately. Then, in a barely audible voice, she said, "The woman in the dark. She's waiting. She doesn't know how to get back."

Sophia's heart hammered in her chest. She felt a lump form in her throat, but she swallowed it down. "It's just a dream, sweetheart. Just a bad dream," she reassured her, though her voice felt strained.

"Can I sleep with the light on, Mama?" Lily's voice cracked.

"Of course," Sophia replied, trying to mask her own rising anxiety. She flicked the switch, bathing the room in soft, golden light.

But as she closed the door and stepped into the hallway, Sophia felt a deep unease settling in her chest, like a weight that wouldn't lift. Was it possible that her daughter, so young and innocent, had somehow tapped into something dark—something beyond her understanding?

The next day, the disturbing behavior continued. Lily's drawings became even more strange and abstract, filled with shadows and distorted images of unfamiliar places. Sophia noticed that her daughter had grown more distant, as though she were drifting between two worlds—one real and one imagined. And though Lily tried to explain the things she saw, Sophia found herself struggling to believe her. It was as if Lily wasn't just creating stories. She was recounting memories.

One afternoon, Sophia arrived home from work to find her daughter standing at the edge of their yard, staring at the trees. The sun was setting, casting long shadows across the grass.

"Lily?" Sophia called softly, her voice wavering slightly as she approached.

Lily didn't turn. She just stood there, as still as a statue, her hands clasped tightly behind her back. "Mama," she said after a long silence. "I remember something else. I remember being afraid... there was a door. A door that I couldn't open. I didn't know how to leave."

Sophia felt a wave of nausea wash over her, but she couldn't move. Lily's words—delivered so calmly, so matter-of-factly—sent a tremor of dread through her. The girl had never spoken like this before. She was describing something... real.

"What do you mean, sweetheart? A door? Where?"

Lily turned her head slightly, her large brown eyes meeting her mother's. "It's like I was trapped. I didn't want to go there. I didn't want to be alone. There was someone... someone who was going to hurt me."

Sophia's knees almost buckled beneath her, but she steadied herself against the fence. She reached for Lily, pulling her into a tight embrace. Her daughter's trembling form in her arms felt like an anchor to reality, but the words Lily spoke seemed to pull her deeper into a nightmare.

Sophia held her tightly, but even as she whispered calming words, her thoughts raced. Could Lily have somehow tapped into something—some memory or presence—far beyond her years? Was it possible that she wasn't simply imagining things?

Sophia wasn't sure anymore. But one thing was clear: this was no ordinary childhood phase. Something was happening, something Sophia couldn't understand—and it was drawing her closer to a mystery that had remained unsolved for years.

Sophia stood in the kitchen that evening, trying to focus on the humdrum task of making dinner. The smell of pasta sauce filled the air, but her mind was far away, tangled in the disquieting events of the past few days. She kept replaying Lily's words in her head—*a door I couldn't open, someone who was going to hurt me.* Those words echoed through her mind like a dark, ominous warning.

The soft hum of the refrigerator was the only sound breaking the silence of the house. Sophia stirred the sauce, her thoughts racing. Was Lily truly experiencing something beyond her comprehension? Or was this just the start of some disturbing phase of her childhood? She couldn't make sense of it. She had always known that being a mother would require patience, but this felt different—this felt like something she couldn't control.

As she set the table, she glanced at the living room, where Lily was sitting on the floor, her legs crossed beneath her. Her daughter was drawing again. There was an eerie quietness about her that Sophia couldn't shake. It wasn't like Lily to be so still. Normally, she was always moving—dancing around the house, asking questions, bouncing off the walls. But tonight, she was silent, almost as though she were in a trance.

Sophia stepped into the living room and crouched down beside her. "Lily, what are you drawing this time?" she asked, trying to keep her voice light. She could already see the shadows creeping in on the page, the same unsettling figures that had started appearing in her daughter's artwork recently.

Lily looked up at her with those wide, dark eyes, and a strange chill ran down Sophia's spine. There was something almost too mature in the way Lily regarded her, a look that didn't belong to an eight-year-old.

"It's the same," Lily said softly, turning the sketchbook toward her mother. "The woman is standing at the door again. She's still waiting."

Sophia's heart thudded in her chest as she looked at the new drawing. The woman in the sketch was now standing in front of a massive, looming door, one that looked ancient and weathered, its edges chipped and cracked. The background was dark, almost black, with jagged shapes that resembled rocky terrain. It was like a scene from a nightmare—an unsettling, impossible image that made Sophia feel as though the room around her was closing in.

Sophia felt the breath catch in her throat. "Lily," she began, her voice trembling slightly. "Who is this woman? Why is she standing at the door?"

Lily's expression remained neutral, but there was an eerie stillness about her. She didn't answer right away. Instead, she stared at the drawing for a long moment, as though lost in thought. When she spoke again, her voice was quiet, almost a whisper.

"She's scared, Mama. She doesn't know how to get through the door. She's trapped. She doesn't belong here, but she's still waiting."

Sophia's chest tightened. A cold, foreboding feeling settled deep inside her. She wanted to ask more questions—about the door, the woman, what Lily was seeing—but something held her back. Part of her was afraid that if she pushed too hard, Lily would say something that would unravel everything, something that would shatter the fragile sense of normalcy they had left.

Instead, Sophia stood up, forcing a smile. "Well, why don't you finish your drawing, and we'll have dinner in a little while?"

Lily nodded without a word, her gaze once again fixed on the page in front of her. As Sophia walked away, she couldn't shake the feeling that her daughter wasn't fully present in the moment—that Lily was somewhere else, somewhere far away, trapped in a world only she could see.

The unsettling thoughts lingered long after dinner. That night, as Sophia tucked Lily into bed, she found herself staring at her daughter, unable to shake the image of the woman in the doorway. The shadows in the room seemed darker, more oppressive than usual, and the light from the nightstand lamp flickered slightly, casting strange, elongated shapes across the walls.

Lily had already pulled the covers up to her chin, but there was a restlessness in her eyes. She shifted uncomfortably under the blankets, her small hands clutching the edge of the sheet.

"Mama," Lily said again, her voice tinged with something Sophia couldn't quite place. It was a feeling, a shift, as though Lily was on the verge of saying something important, something that would change everything.

Sophia leaned down, brushing a strand of hair from Lily's face. "What is it, sweetheart?"

Lily's voice dropped to a whisper, barely audible. "I'm scared, Mama. The woman... she's still there. I don't want her to come inside. She's looking for me. She's coming."

Sophia froze, a wave of cold running through her veins. She wanted to say something, to reassure her daughter, to tell her that it was just a bad dream or an overactive imagination. But the words stuck in her throat.

Before she could respond, Lily sat up suddenly, her eyes wide with fear. "Mama, she's here. I saw her again."

Sophia's heart skipped a beat, and she grabbed Lily's hand, pulling her close. "Lily, it's just a dream. There's nothing to be afraid of, sweetheart. Just sleep now. Everything will be okay."

But Lily wasn't listening. Her eyes were fixed on the corner of the room, staring as though she saw something Sophia couldn't.

"She's waiting," Lily repeated in a soft, distant voice. "She's waiting for you."

Sophia's heart sank into her chest. She didn't know whether to feel fear or concern, but her protective instincts kicked in. She couldn't let Lily go on like this. She needed answers. But no matter how much she wanted to reach out to her daughter, to hold her, she felt a growing sense of helplessness. Something was happening to Lily—something she couldn't explain—and it terrified her.

Sophia squeezed her daughter's hand and whispered, "It's okay. I'm here, and I'll keep you safe. Always." But even as the words left her mouth, she wasn't sure she believed them herself.

As she sat there in the dim light, holding her daughter close, she couldn't shake the feeling that they were both standing at the edge of something much darker than she could understand. Something that went beyond the boundaries of this world.

Sophia lay awake long after she had tucked Lily into bed, staring at the ceiling in the darkness of their quiet house. The strange, troubling images her daughter had described—especially the recurring figure of the woman at the door—refused to leave her mind. She couldn't shake the feeling that this wasn't just a figment of Lily's imagination. There was something undeniably real about it.

She had tried to reason with herself: children have vivid dreams, sometimes even hallucinations, especially when they are under stress or going through a developmental phase. But this... this felt different. The conviction in Lily's voice, the fear in her eyes, the way she seemed to be seeing something that Sophia couldn't—none of it made sense.

Sophia turned over, glancing at the clock on her nightstand. It was nearly 2 a.m., and she was still wide awake, her mind racing. She knew she needed to do something about this. But what?

She had already called Lily's pediatrician that afternoon, but the doctor had assured her that it was just a phase, that children sometimes go through periods of imaginary friends or odd behavior. The reassurance had done little to calm Sophia's nerves.

Sighing, she decided to check on Lily again, just to make sure she was okay. It wasn't uncommon for her daughter to have nightmares, but tonight felt different. Something was off, and Sophia couldn't ignore it.

Quietly, she slipped out of bed, trying not to wake her husband, Thomas, who was snoring softly beside her. She padded down the hallway and stopped in front of Lily's bedroom door, which was slightly ajar.

The moonlight from the window filtered in, casting long, eerie shadows across the floor. The house was silent—too silent. Sophia opened the door and peered inside.

Lily was sitting up in bed again, just like before, her small figure hunched over. She seemed completely still, as though she were in a trance. Her wide eyes were fixed on the corner of the room, just as they had been earlier.

"Mama," Lily whispered without turning around, her voice hollow, almost robotic. "She's here. I told you she was coming."

Sophia's heart lurched. She slowly approached the bed, her pulse quickening. "Lily, it's okay. You're just dreaming. It's all in your head."

But Lily didn't respond to her mother's voice. She didn't even seem to notice Sophia's presence in the room. Her gaze remained locked on the corner.

Sophia felt a cold shiver run down her spine. She could no longer deny it—something wasn't right. Her daughter wasn't just imagining things. There was something going on here, something she wasn't ready to confront.

"Lily," Sophia said, trying to sound calm, though her voice trembled. "Come on, sweetheart. Let's lie down and get some rest."

Lily slowly turned her head toward her mother. Her eyes were wide and glassy, unblinking. There was no recognition in them, no sign that she was even truly present in the room with Sophia. It was like she was somewhere else entirely, lost in a different world.

Sophia sat down next to her, her mind racing. She wasn't sure what she expected Lily to say next, but the words that came from her daughter's lips struck terror into her heart.

"She's waiting for you, Mama. She's been looking for you all this time," Lily whispered, her voice barely audible. "She's going to take you through the door. She'll show you everything."

Sophia felt a cold, sickening fear settle deep in her stomach. She wanted to scream, to shake her daughter out of whatever trance she was in, but something in her gut told her that this wasn't just a bad dream. This was something far darker, something much more dangerous than she could possibly understand.

Suddenly, Lily blinked and looked at her mother as if waking from a fog. Her eyes softened, and the trance-like quality left her expression.

"Mama?" she asked, her voice small and innocent once more.

Sophia tried to steady her breathing. "Yes, sweetheart. It's me. Are you okay?"

Lily nodded slowly, though she looked confused, as if unsure of what had just happened. "I—I don't know. I feel... strange."

Sophia pulled her into a hug, pressing her face into Lily's soft hair. "You're okay, Lily. It's just a bad dream. Let's go back to sleep."

But Sophia wasn't convinced. She didn't know if it was a dream at all. She didn't know what was happening to her daughter, and that scared her more than anything.

As she lay back down beside Lily, cradling her close, she stared at the ceiling, her mind swirling with questions. Was this just the start of something? Had Lily been touched by something beyond their world—something supernatural? Or was it something else entirely, something more grounded in reality?

But before she could ask herself any more questions, she felt the subtle shift of Lily's body against hers. She could tell that her daughter had fallen asleep again, her breathing slow and steady.

Sophia wasn't sure what she believed anymore, but the fact that Lily had mentioned *the door* again—the same one that had appeared in her drawings—was enough to make her skin crawl. What if the woman Lily saw wasn't just a figment of her imagination, but something much darker?

Sophia closed her eyes, trying to push the thought from her mind, but it wouldn't go away. Whatever this was, it was only just beginning.

The next morning, Sophia tried to push the events of the previous night to the back of her mind. It was hard to shake off the image of Lily's eerie stare, the vacant expression on her daughter's face as she spoke of the mysterious woman and the door. But when morning came, the sun filtering through the curtains, everything seemed almost normal again. The world outside their little home continued on as usual. Birds chirped outside the window, and the hum of distant traffic sounded like an ordinary morning.

Sophia moved around the kitchen, preparing breakfast for Lily and Thomas. As she cracked eggs into the pan, she tried to convince herself that it had all been a bad dream. Children had vivid imaginations, especially when they were under stress. It could be that Lily's mind had created this image of the woman—perhaps she had seen a picture or heard a story somewhere.

"Mom!" Lily's voice interrupted her thoughts, and Sophia turned to find her standing in the doorway of the kitchen, clutching her stuffed bunny.

Lily had a strange look in her eyes, an expression that Sophia couldn't quite place. It was as if she were holding something back—something important, but she wasn't sure how to say it.

"What is it, sweetheart?" Sophia asked, wiping her hands on a towel and moving toward her daughter.

Lily hesitated for a moment, then said, "I saw her again last night. The woman. She was watching me."

Sophia felt a chill spread through her chest. She had been hoping, praying, that it was just a one-off experience, but the fact that Lily was still talking about it, still seeing this woman, made it harder to ignore.

Sophia knelt down to Lily's level, her hands resting on her daughter's small shoulders. "Lily, you know that wasn't real, right? It was just a dream."

Lily shook her head. "It wasn't a dream, Mama. I see her when I wake up too. She's in the corner of the room, always looking at me, waiting for me."

Sophia's heart pounded in her chest. "What do you mean, waiting for you?"

Lily's face twisted with confusion. "I don't know. I think she wants me to go with her... through the door."

The room seemed to grow colder as Lily spoke those words. "Through the door." Sophia felt her stomach turn. She couldn't understand what Lily was trying to tell her, but the more she heard, the more certain she became that there was something more to this than just a child's imagination.

Suddenly, the sound of the front door opening interrupted their conversation. Thomas entered the kitchen, his face tired but smiling. He kissed Sophia on the cheek and set his briefcase down on the counter.

"Morning, love," he said cheerfully, before turning to Lily. "How's my girl today?"

Lily looked up at her father, her face lighting up for a brief moment, but then her expression quickly darkened again. "Daddy, the woman is still here."

Thomas stopped in his tracks, his smile fading slightly as he looked at Sophia for an explanation.

Sophia's mind raced, but she didn't know what to say. She couldn't explain the fear that had settled in her gut, nor could she bring herself to tell Thomas what Lily had been saying. He would think she was overreacting or worrying too much, especially since he hadn't witnessed the strange occurrences for himself.

Thomas crouched down to Lily's level. "What woman, honey? We talked about this. It's probably just a bad dream."

Lily shook her head, her expression serious and unwavering. "She's real, Daddy. She's waiting for me."

Sophia felt a lump form in her throat. She could see the tension building on Thomas's face. He was trying to remain calm, but there was a flicker of doubt in his eyes. He was beginning to question whether this was just some harmless phase or something more unsettling.

Sophia took a deep breath and decided it was time to confront the issue head-on. She had to get to the bottom of this before it consumed them both.

"I think we need to talk to someone," she said firmly, looking at Thomas. "A therapist, maybe? Someone who can help us figure out what's going on with Lily. This isn't just a phase anymore."

Thomas's brow furrowed. "Are you sure? You think she needs therapy? Maybe we should just wait and see if it passes."

Sophia shook her head. "No, I think we need to take it seriously. There's something strange happening, and I can't just ignore it anymore."

Thomas was silent for a moment, then nodded slowly. "Okay. If you think it'll help."

Sophia felt a small sense of relief. She wasn't sure what exactly she was expecting therapy to reveal, but it felt like a step in the right direction. It would be something tangible, something concrete that they could do to try and understand what was happening to their daughter.

After breakfast, Sophia made an appointment with a child psychologist. It felt like the right thing to do, but as the hours passed, the dread only grew. What if the psychologist couldn't help them? What if this was something beyond their understanding, something that no professional could explain?

That evening, as Sophia tucked Lily into bed, she kissed her daughter's forehead and tried to comfort her. But Lily's eyes were wide and unblinking, staring up at the ceiling as though she was waiting for something—or someone.

"Mama," Lily whispered, her voice small and anxious. "Is she going to take me through the door tonight?"

Sophia's heart sank. She tried to smile, to reassure her daughter, but the fear that Lily's words carried made it almost impossible. "No, sweetheart. You're safe here. The woman can't take you anywhere. You're just having dreams."

But even as she said the words, Sophia couldn't escape the nagging feeling that it wasn't just a dream. Something else was happening. And she was afraid they were running out of time to stop it.

The days that followed became increasingly strained. Sophia couldn't shake the growing sense of unease that lingered in their home. It wasn't just Lily's behavior anymore. The air itself seemed to carry a heaviness, an unspoken tension that Sophia couldn't explain. Even simple tasks like making dinner or reading to Lily at night felt burdened by an underlying fear.

Lily's strange episodes continued, and with each passing day, Sophia noticed more unsettling details. Sometimes Lily would sit in the same spot for hours, staring at the same corner of the room, her bunny clutched tightly in her arms. At other times, she would suddenly start talking to someone who wasn't there. "Mama, she's here again," Lily would say, her voice distant, her eyes locked onto something in the room only she could see.

Sophia tried to be patient, telling herself that children had vivid imaginations. But there were moments when she couldn't ignore the growing fear in Lily's eyes, the way she seemed so certain that there was something—someone—watching her. It wasn't just a child's fantasy anymore. It felt real. And that thought terrified Sophia.

One evening, as they were winding down for bed, Thomas came to Sophia with a concerned look on his face. He had been unusually quiet all day, and she could sense that he was beginning to feel the weight of the situation too.

"I think we need to do more than just talk to a therapist," Thomas said quietly, his voice filled with a quiet desperation. "I can't keep pretending this is nothing."

Sophia's heart skipped a beat. "What do you mean?"

Thomas paced the living room, running a hand through his hair. "I don't know, but it's like I can feel it too now. Whatever is going on with Lily... it's not just in her head. I've been thinking about the stories we've heard—about people who've gone missing, about the things people say after they come back from... whatever it is that happens to them. I don't know. It just doesn't feel like something that can be solved with therapy. We need to understand what's going on. We need to find answers."

Sophia's stomach twisted. "What do you mean? You think it's something bigger than what we've been told?"

"I don't know yet, but it feels like it's all connected. The woman, the door, the things Lily's been saying. It's like she knows something... something we don't."

Sophia nodded slowly, her mind racing with the implications. Could there be something more to Lily's visions? She had been reluctant to consider it, but now, with Thomas's words hanging heavily in the air, she couldn't deny the possibility.

"I'll make some calls tomorrow," she said, though her voice felt hollow. "We'll figure this out."

That night, Sophia couldn't sleep. She tossed and turned, her mind swirling with doubts and fears. She kept seeing the same image in her head: the door that Lily kept talking about, the one that seemed to beckon her. And then there was the woman—Clara Bennett, the missing person whose name had been in the news years ago. Was it possible that Lily was somehow connected to her? That this strange, eerie presence in their lives was tied to something far beyond their understanding?

It was a question that gnawed at Sophia's mind, one that she couldn't shake no matter how hard she tried.

The next morning, Sophia did what she had promised. She contacted the psychologist they had seen the previous week and explained the situation in more detail. The doctor was kind but firm, telling her that it was important to explore every possibility. But Sophia could sense that even the psychologist didn't have all the answers. There were too many unknowns. The more Sophia delved into this strange reality, the more she realized how little she truly understood.

Later that afternoon, as she sat in the living room with Lily, the doorbell rang. Sophia wasn't expecting anyone, and the timing made her uneasy. She opened the door to find a woman standing on the porch, holding a brown envelope.

"Ms. Reed?" the woman asked, her voice soft but authoritative.

Sophia nodded, confused. "Yes, can I help you?"

The woman extended the envelope. "I have something for you. It's about your daughter."

Sophia felt her heart race. "What is this? Who are you?"

The woman hesitated for a moment, then said, "I'm a private investigator. I've been looking into the case of Clara Bennett. I think you and your daughter might be connected to her disappearance."

Sophia's breath caught in her throat. "What do you mean?"

The woman lowered her voice. "Please, let me explain inside. It's better if we talk privately."

Sophia looked down at Lily, who was standing by the door, her eyes wide. There was something about the way Lily was staring at the woman that sent a shiver down Sophia's spine. It was like she recognized her, like she knew her already. The feeling of unease deepened, and Sophia nodded, stepping aside to let the woman in.

As they sat down in the living room, the investigator began to explain. "Clara Bennett disappeared several years ago under mysterious circumstances. Her case has remained unsolved, but there have been rumors about her possible connection to children, children who may have been reincarnated or who have somehow been involved in the case in some way. I've been investigating this theory, and the more I looked into it, the more I found connections—connections that led me to your daughter."

Sophia's head spun. "What connections? How could Lily be involved in something like this?"

The investigator paused, then slid a folder across the table to Sophia. Inside were newspaper clippings, photographs, and a map. Clara Bennett's face stared back at Sophia, hauntingly familiar.

"This is Clara," the investigator said. "But there's something else you need to know. We've found that children like your daughter, children with memories or visions of past lives, often have experiences that link them to people who are no longer alive. I believe your daughter may be the key to uncovering what happened to Clara."

Sophia's mind raced. Was this all just a coincidence? Or was Lily truly connected to the mysterious disappearance of Clara Bennett? And if so, what did it mean for their family? What was the truth behind the strange occurrences, the woman in the corner of the room, and the door that Lily kept mentioning?

As Sophia stared at the photographs in front of her, she felt a cold wave of realization wash over her. This was no longer just a mother's worry over her child's strange behavior. This was something far darker, far more complex than she could have ever imagined. And they were only just beginning to uncover the truth.

Chapter Two: Fragments of the Unknown

Part One: The First Sketch

It had been three days since the investigator's visit, and though the conversation still haunted Sophia's mind, she had tried to carry on with life as best she could. The days since the meeting had grown colder, and the air in the house seemed heavier, almost as if the walls themselves were holding their breath.

Lily had become increasingly distant, retreating into her world of quiet observation. It was as if she had withdrawn from everything around her, her once vibrant energy muted. Sophia could no longer simply chalk up Lily's odd behavior to childhood imagination. The weight of the situation pressed down on her with every passing day.

It was late in the afternoon when Sophia first noticed the sketches. She had been in the kitchen preparing dinner when Lily, who had been sitting at the small wooden table near the window, suddenly began to draw. At first, Sophia didn't think much of it. It was a common enough sight—Lily loved to sketch, her crayons and colored pencils scattered across the table, bringing to life a host of fantastical creatures, dreamlike scenes, and images from stories Sophia had told her. But this time, there was something different about it. The way Lily held the pencil was tighter, more deliberate, as though she were trying to capture something urgent, something pressing.

Sophia wiped her hands on a dish towel, approaching the table cautiously. "What are you drawing, sweetheart?" she asked gently.

Lily didn't respond at first, her brow furrowed in deep concentration. After a long moment, she looked up at her mother, her eyes distant, as if seeing something far beyond the walls of their home. She handed Sophia the page. The drawing was of a door, stark and unremarkable at first glance, but something about it felt off. It was a door that didn't belong in the room. Its edges were smudged, and the handle was unusually detailed. A faint mist seemed to rise from the base of the door, blurring the edges of the image.

Sophia's breath caught in her throat. It looked like the very door Lily had mentioned before—the one she had been speaking about in her strange, cryptic ramblings. The same door that had seemed to call to her. But this was more than just an idle drawing. It was as though Lily was compelled to capture it.

"Where did you see this, Lily?" Sophia asked, her voice trembling slightly.

Lily didn't answer. Instead, she simply pointed to the drawing, her tiny finger hovering above the mist. "It's behind the door," she said softly.

Sophia's heart raced. Behind the door? The words lingered in the room like an echo, leaving a coldness in their wake.

Without another word, Sophia took the sketch and placed it in a drawer, trying to shake the creeping sense of unease that gnawed at her. Was it possible that Lily's imagination had simply run wild? Or was there something more sinister at play?

As Sophia finished preparing dinner, she found it difficult to shake the image of the door from her mind. It had felt too real. Too familiar. And as much as she wanted to dismiss it as just another drawing, another child's flight of fancy, she couldn't. Something was wrong. Her daughter had seen something—something that neither of them fully understood.

Part Two: The Phrase That Haunts

The next day, Sophia noticed something else. Lily had taken to speaking in fragments, strange, disjointed phrases that seemed to have no clear connection to reality. She wasn't speaking in full sentences anymore, and her voice often seemed as though it were coming from somewhere far away. The words she muttered didn't make sense, but their weight felt too real to ignore.

That afternoon, as Sophia was tidying up the living room, she overheard Lily talking to herself in the next room. The phrases she was speaking made Sophia's skin crawl.

"He watches... always watching... the man with the glass eyes..." Lily whispered, her voice low and trembling.

Sophia froze in her tracks. Glass eyes? The phrase was one Sophia had never heard before. Was it from a book? A story? But Lily had never mentioned anything like it.

Sophia took a hesitant step forward, peering around the corner. Lily was sitting on the floor, playing with her toy blocks, but there was something different in her demeanor. Her back was stiff, her movements stiff and mechanical. She appeared oblivious to her mother's presence, her attention fixed on something unseen.

"He waits," Lily continued, her voice distant. "He'll come when the clock strikes."

Sophia's blood ran cold. The clock? Was Lily referring to a specific time? And who was this mysterious figure with glass eyes? Was she describing someone she had seen—or was this just a figment of her imagination? Or was it something far more sinister?

Sophia couldn't contain the questions that flooded her mind. She had to know what Lily was talking about, had to understand what was going on inside her daughter's head. But no matter how many times she tried to ask, Lily simply clammed up, staring at the floor or looking out the window as if lost in a world only she could see.

Later that evening, as Sophia was about to tuck Lily into bed, she noticed something even more troubling. Lily had drawn another picture—this one more disturbing than the last.

It was of a man. A man with unnaturally dark, hollow eyes. His face was gaunt, his features sharp, and his expression was one of cold indifference. There was a shadow in the background of the drawing, an oppressive darkness that seemed to engulf the figure. The man's hands were raised as if he were holding something invisible. And behind him, at the far edge of the drawing, was the same door—a door that seemed to loom larger than the man, a door that felt like a gateway to something beyond comprehension.

Sophia's hands shook as she held the drawing. This wasn't just a child's innocent scribble. This was something far darker, far more ominous. And Lily was drawing it over and over again, each image more vivid, more detailed than the last.

"What is this, Lily?" Sophia asked gently, though she was afraid to hear the answer.

Lily didn't answer immediately. She simply stared at the drawing, her face pale. Then, in a voice barely above a whisper, she spoke. "The man with the glass eyes... He's waiting behind the door."

The words struck Sophia like a blow. It was the same man, the same door. And in that moment, she understood—whatever Lily was seeing, whatever was happening to her, was not just a figment of her imagination. Something, or someone, was trying to communicate with her. And whatever it was, it was no longer content to stay in the shadows.

Part Three: The Growing Presence

That night, as Sophia lay awake in bed, staring at the ceiling, she couldn't shake the feeling that something was watching her. The house, usually a place of comfort, now felt cold, its walls closing in on her. She couldn't remember when it had started, this suffocating sense of being observed, but it was there, lurking in the corners of her mind, pulling her deeper into a world she couldn't understand.

The next morning, she returned to the sketches. There were more now, scattered across Lily's room. Some were hastily drawn, others more meticulous. Some seemed to depict people, others objects. But each one had one thing in common—the door. In every single drawing, the door was present. It was always there, standing ominously at the center of each scene. And more disturbingly, there were now figures surrounding it, figures that looked like shadows—like something trapped in the dark, waiting to emerge.

Sophia's eyes scanned the drawings in a daze. The air around her seemed to thicken, the weight of the unknown pressing down on her chest. What was Lily trying to tell her? What was this door that kept appearing in every image? And why had Lily begun to speak of things that no child should know?

Sophia's fear deepened as she realized the magnitude of what she was dealing with. These weren't just random scribbles. They were fragments—fragments of something much larger, much darker, and much more dangerous than she had ever imagined.

Part Four: The Nightmares Begin

The dreams started two nights later, and they were not ordinary nightmares. They were vivid and disjointed, filled with images of a foggy, dimly lit room. In the center of this room stood the door. The same door Lily had drawn, the same door that had haunted Sophia's thoughts ever since she first saw it. But in the dreams, it was more than just a drawing. It was alive, pulsating, as if it held a presence, a beating heart that resonated within the walls.

In her dream, Sophia walked toward the door, each step feeling heavier than the last. The air was thick with an otherworldly silence, and as she reached for the doorknob, a cold chill rushed over her. She could hear Lily's voice calling to her from behind the door, faint at first, but growing clearer with each moment.

"Mom," Lily's voice echoed through the fog, distant yet urgent, "don't open it..."

But Sophia's hand was already on the handle. She couldn't resist. She turned it slowly, and as the door creaked open, a darkness far deeper than the night itself spilled out. It was a darkness that felt alive—like it was waiting for her, drawing her in. Sophia tried to pull away, but her hand remained fixed to the knob, as if some invisible force was keeping her in place.

When she woke up, gasping for breath, the feeling of dread lingered, sticking to her skin like the damp air of the dream. She was covered in sweat, her heart racing. But it wasn't just the nightmare that unsettled her—it was the sense of déjà vu that clung to her. It felt like she had been there before. Like she had lived that moment countless times, in some parallel reality.

When Sophia opened her eyes to find Lily standing in the doorway of her bedroom, watching her, she felt a shiver run down her spine. Her daughter's expression was distant, unreadable.

"I saw you, Mom," Lily whispered, her voice soft, but the words carried a weight, as if they were too heavy for her small frame. "You were at the door."

Sophia's throat tightened. How could Lily know? It wasn't possible. But the look in Lily's eyes told her that the boundaries between dreams and reality were beginning to blur.

"I didn't open it," Sophia whispered back, trying to reassure herself. But the words felt hollow.

Lily didn't answer. She only stared at her mother, the same vacant look in her eyes as when she had spoken of the man with glass eyes. She then turned and walked away, her footsteps light but deliberate, as if she were being drawn toward something unseen.

Sophia sat in bed for a long time, her mind racing. Was Lily seeing the same things she was? Or was something else reaching out to her daughter, pulling her into a reality she couldn't understand? And what about the door? What was it, really? Was it merely a figment of their imagination, or something far more dangerous?

Sophia could no longer ignore the growing terror that had taken root in her heart. There was a connection between Lily's drawings, her words, and these dreams. Something was happening—something that felt like it was beyond their control.

Part Five: The Inexplicable Incident

The following afternoon, things took an even darker turn. Sophia had left Lily in the living room while she stepped outside to check the mail. When she returned, her heart stopped at the sight of what awaited her.

The living room, usually calm and orderly, was in complete disarray. The furniture had been overturned, books were scattered across the floor, and the curtains were drawn tight, casting the room in an eerie, oppressive darkness. It wasn't the kind of mess that a child might make during play—it was something far more chaotic, far more deliberate.

Sophia rushed into the room, calling Lily's name, her voice trembling. But Lily wasn't there. Panic crept into her chest as she searched the house, calling out for her daughter, her voice rising in desperation.

"Lily!" she cried, her breath quickening. "Where are you?"

She was about to check the basement when she heard a soft rustling from the kitchen. Turning sharply, she rushed toward the sound, her heart pounding in her chest. There, sitting in the corner of the room, was Lily.

But she wasn't herself. Her eyes were wide, unblinking, her body stiff as though she were frozen in place. She was holding something in her hands—a piece of paper. Another drawing.

Sophia's heart sank as she approached her daughter. Lily didn't look up, didn't react in any way. She remained frozen, her grip tight around the paper, her eyes locked on the blank space in front of her.

"Lily?" Sophia whispered, her voice hoarse. She reached out, gently pulling the drawing from Lily's hands. As soon as she did, Lily blinked, the trance breaking. She looked up at her mother, her face blank, as though the last few moments had been a dream.

"Lily, what's going on?" Sophia asked, her voice shaking. "Why did you do this?"

Lily didn't answer. She simply stared at the paper in Sophia's hands, her gaze distant and unfocused.

Sophia's hands trembled as she unfurled the drawing. It was another picture of the door—this time, however, it was different. The door wasn't just a door anymore. There was a face emerging from it, a twisted, contorted face with hollow, glassy eyes. It was the same face Lily had mentioned in her strange mutterings. The face that haunted her dreams. And as Sophia looked at the paper, she felt a chill spread through her chest, as if the door itself were looking back at her, beckoning her closer.

This was no longer just a child's fantasy. This was a warning.

Part Six: The Search for Answers

The following days were filled with a sense of urgency. Sophia couldn't ignore the growing feeling that something was terribly wrong. She needed answers, and she needed them fast.

The first step was visiting the local library. She knew she had to research anything that could shed light on Lily's behavior—on the door, on the figure with the glass eyes, and on the strange drawings and phrases that had become a daily occurrence. She had already spoken to a therapist, but the answers she received had been vague, unhelpful. Now, she was on her own, determined to uncover the truth.

As she sat in the library's quiet reading area, flipping through old books on folklore, myth, and paranormal phenomena, a name kept surfacing—Clara Bennett. The more Sophia read about her, the more unsettling the connections became. Clara had vanished under mysterious circumstances several years ago, and rumors had circulated that her disappearance had been linked to strange occurrences, particularly with a young child who had claimed to have visions of Clara's last moments.

The details of Clara's disappearance were sparse, but one thing was clear: the strange visions described by the child who had witnessed Clara's last days mirrored Lily's behavior in disturbing ways. And what was even more chilling was the mention of a door—an old, weathered door that was said to be the key to unlocking the mystery of Clara Bennett's disappearance.

Sophia's hands began to shake as she read through the article, the pieces of the puzzle slowly coming together in her mind. Could it be? Could Lily somehow be connected to Clara Bennett, the missing woman? Was her daughter truly experiencing the same haunting visions that had once gripped the child who had been linked to Clara's vanishing?

With dread settling deep in her gut, Sophia knew that the answers she was seeking were far darker and more dangerous than she had ever imagined. She was no longer just trying to protect her daughter from a bad dream. She was racing against time to uncover the truth before it was too late.

Part Seven: The Stranger's Visit

The next evening, just after sunset, as the house settled into the silence of twilight, there came a knock at the door. It was strange, unsettling—an unfamiliar sound in an otherwise quiet neighborhood. Sophia hesitated before going to answer, her mind already on edge from the days of strange events.

Opening the door, she found a man standing on the porch. He was tall, his face obscured by a wide-brimmed hat, casting a shadow over his features. He wore a long, dark coat, and there was something about his posture, something deliberate and careful, that sent an immediate shiver down Sophia's spine.

"Can I help you?" she asked cautiously, her voice soft yet firm. She had no idea who this man was or how he had come to know her address, and she couldn't shake the feeling that something was not quite right.

The man didn't immediately speak. Instead, his gaze flicked past Sophia, his eyes briefly lingering on the interior of the house. A fleeting look, but one that made Sophia's heart race. He turned his attention back to her.

"I'm looking for someone," he said, his voice deep, resonating in a way that seemed to echo in the stillness around them. His eyes locked onto hers, cold and calculating. "A little girl named Lily."

Sophia felt a chill run through her body. "Who are you?" she demanded, her protective instincts kicking in. "How do you know her name?"

The man didn't answer at first, only stepped closer, just enough for the dim light to reveal a faint smile on his lips. But it wasn't a smile that comforted her. It was the kind of smile that made her skin crawl—faintly sinister, unreadable.

"I'm... a friend of hers," he said finally, though the words seemed hollow. "I've been looking for her."

Sophia stiffened, instinctively stepping forward, blocking the doorway. "You need to leave."

The smile faded, replaced by an unreadable expression. The man took a step back but did not retreat completely, as though his presence was an unwanted but necessary element in some larger game. He nodded once, a slight gesture that seemed to convey his acknowledgment of her demand.

"Be careful," he said cryptically, his eyes narrowing, a flicker of something dark passing through them. "The door calls to her. It calls to all of us."

Before Sophia could respond, before she could even react, the man turned and walked away. He moved with a strange grace, almost as if he were floating just above the ground. Sophia stood frozen for a moment, unsure of what she had just witnessed. The words he had spoken echoed in her mind, the weight of them settling in her stomach like a stone.

The door. What door?

Lily had drawn the door. She had been obsessed with it. But what could this stranger—this man who knew her name—possibly know about it? And what did he mean by the door calling to her? To them?

Sophia shut the door with a firm thud, her heart racing. She leaned against it for a moment, trying to collect her thoughts. But the moment she turned around, she froze.

Lily was standing just at the edge of the hallway, watching her silently, her face pale, her expression unreadable.

"Who was that?" Sophia asked, her voice strained.

Lily didn't answer right away. Instead, she took a step forward, her gaze distant as if she were caught in a memory she couldn't escape. "He's coming," she whispered. "He's here."

Sophia's blood ran cold. "Lily, who is he? What do you mean?"

Lily's lips trembled slightly, but she didn't speak again. She simply walked past her mother and into her room, the sound of her small feet eerily quiet against the hardwood floors.

Sophia stood frozen, unsure of what to make of the situation. The cryptic encounter with the stranger, Lily's disturbing behavior, and the words that hung heavy in the air... The man had said the door called to her, but how could he have known that? Was it just coincidence? Or was something far more sinister happening?

PART EIGHT: THE RETURN of the Sketches

That night, after the strange encounter, Sophia couldn't shake the sense of foreboding that clung to her. It wasn't just the stranger's visit—it was everything. Lily's drawings, the cryptic words she muttered in her sleep, the unsettling dreams Sophia herself was having.

Around midnight, unable to sleep, Sophia found herself standing in the living room, staring at the sketches Lily had made. They were pinned up on the wall now, framed like some twisted gallery of horror. The door, the man with glass eyes, the eerie faces peering out from behind the wooden planks—all of it was laid out before her.

Sophia's gaze was drawn to one sketch in particular, one that was newer than the others. It was a drawing of a face—distorted, almost grotesque. The eyes were hollow, like the black voids of a creature that existed in the dark corners of the world. The features were elongated and stretched, with a sinister grin that seemed to reach too far across the page.

Sophia's hand trembled as she reached out to touch it, but just as her fingers brushed the surface, a noise made her freeze. A soft, almost inaudible tapping sound. It came from the direction of Lily's room.

Sophia stood still, listening, her heart thudding in her chest. The tapping came again. Faint. Purposeful. Like someone, or something, was trying to get her attention.

She hesitated, then moved toward the sound, the air around her thick with tension. She opened the door to Lily's room and found her daughter sitting up in bed, wide-eyed, her face pale.

Lily wasn't speaking. She was simply staring at the wall, her fingers twitching slightly as if she were in a trance. Sophia's heart skipped a beat.

"What is it, Lily?" she asked softly, afraid of the answer.

Lily turned slowly, her gaze distant, unfocused. "The door's calling," she whispered. "It won't let me sleep."

Sophia's breath caught in her throat. Lily had mentioned the door again. It wasn't just a fleeting thought—Lily was fixated on it. But it was more than that. It was as if the door had become a living thing, something that exerted a pull on her daughter, something that she couldn't escape.

Sophia moved to her daughter's side, trying to calm her. But even as she stroked Lily's hair and whispered soothing words, she felt it—the unease, the heaviness in the air. She wasn't sure what was happening, but she knew one thing for certain: things were spiraling out of control.

The door was no longer just a symbol. It was a manifestation of something much darker, something that had already begun to sink its claws into their lives.

PART NINE: UNEARTHED Secrets

The next morning, Sophia decided to confront the past—specifically, the mystery of Clara Bennett's disappearance. She couldn't shake the feeling that this was the key to everything that was happening with Lily. The cryptic drawings, the strange behavior, the man who had come to their doorstep... it all seemed to connect to Clara's vanishing.

Sophia spent the entire day poring over old police reports, newspaper clippings, and any information she could find about Clara. The more she read, the more certain she became that there was a hidden truth buried beneath the surface.

Clara Bennett had been a young woman, full of promise, with a bright future ahead of her. But everything had changed when she had started experiencing strange visions—visions of a door, of an unknown place that seemed to beckon her. According to the reports, Clara had been seen drawing the door, much like Lily. She had become obsessed with it, just as Lily was now.

And then, one day, Clara had disappeared. No one knew where she had gone, but there were whispers. Whispers about the door. Whispers about something far darker at play.

Sophia's hand shook as she flipped through the final report, a single sentence standing out: "The door was the key. But some doors are not meant to be opened."

Sophia felt a cold rush of fear flood through her. She had no idea what was happening, but she knew it had something to do with that door. And now, Lily was entangled in it, whether she realized it or not.

As Sophia sat there, contemplating the connection, she knew one thing for certain: she had to protect her daughter. No matter what it took, she would do whatever was necessary to keep Lily safe from whatever lay behind that door.

But what if the door had already started to claim her?

Chapter Three: Secrets in the Past

Part One: A Mother's Determination

Sophia sat at the kitchen table, surrounded by a mountain of old newspapers, police reports, and photos that she had pulled from various archives. The weight of the past bore down on her as she sifted through each document, looking for any clue that might explain the strange connection between Clara Bennett's disappearance and her daughter's recent behavior. The more she read, the more she felt like she was entering a world she couldn't understand, but one she had no choice but to explore.

Clara Bennett had been a young woman—a mother, just like Sophia—when she vanished without a trace. Her disappearance had shocked the town, and despite the years that had passed, there was still an air of mystery surrounding her case. The police had never found Clara, and they had eventually declared her missing, presumed dead. The only thing that remained were the scattered reports and whispered rumors that spoke of a strange obsession with a mysterious door before she disappeared.

Sophia's heart pounded as she came across an old interview with one of Clara's closest friends. The woman, now in her late fifties, spoke about Clara's obsession with drawings and visions. Clara had claimed that she was seeing a door—a door that seemed to call to her. Sophia froze, a cold chill running through her veins. That same door had appeared in Lily's sketches. Lily had spoken of it in her sleep. Was this a coincidence?

"No," Sophia whispered to herself. "This can't be just a coincidence."

Her mind raced. Was Lily somehow connected to Clara? Could this be the reason Lily was behaving so strangely? Was her daughter somehow channeling Clara's lost soul, or was something far darker at play?

Part Two: Drawing the Connection

Sophia spent the next few days in a whirlwind of research, poring over the same documents, piecing together Clara's fragmented life. The parallels between Clara's obsession with the door and Lily's recent behavior were too striking to ignore. Clara had drawn the door incessantly, just as Lily had done. And then, just like Lily, Clara had started to speak of the door—though she had described it as something that whispered to her in her dreams, calling her, pulling her toward it.

The more Sophia uncovered, the more unsettling it became. Clara had become withdrawn, detached from her friends and family, as if the door consumed her very soul. Her friends recalled her speaking in cryptic phrases, talking about a place she called "The Other Side." Sophia's stomach tightened as she read these words. Lily had used similar phrases. The Other Side. Was it possible that Clara had known something about the door, something that had driven her to vanish?

Sophia's fingers trembled as she flipped through the pages, her eyes landing on a particularly haunting entry. A final entry from Clara's diary, dated just days before her disappearance: *"I can feel it now, the door. It's opening, and I can't stop it. It's calling to me, pulling me into the dark. I can't escape. I'm afraid of what will happen when I step through. But I have to go."*

The words were like a scream that echoed in the stillness of the room. Sophia felt her breath catch in her throat. Clara had known something. She had felt something terrible—something that had driven her to the edge. And now, it seemed, that same force was calling to Lily. Was her daughter being drawn into the same dark fate?

Sophia slammed the diary shut, her heart hammering in her chest. She could no longer ignore the mounting evidence that something sinister was at work. Clara's obsession with the door was no accident, and neither was Lily's.

Part Three: A Mother's Fear

Later that night, after Lily had gone to bed, Sophia found herself standing at the edge of the darkened hallway, staring at her daughter's door. She had tried to reassure herself that it was just a phase—that Lily's behavior was nothing more than the result of an overactive imagination. But deep down, Sophia knew that wasn't the case. Something far darker was at play, and the more she uncovered, the more terrifying the truth became.

Lily's sketches had become more detailed over the past week, the images growing more unsettling with each new drawing. The door was no longer just a simple doorway—it had become something more. Something sinister. The figures in her sketches had taken on a life of their own, their expressions twisted with anguish and desperation. Some of the figures appeared to be clawing at the door, their hands reaching out as if trying to escape. Others stood silently, their eyes hollow and vacant, as though they had been trapped on the other side for an eternity.

Sophia's mind raced. Was Lily seeing these things in her dreams? Or was there something more to her drawings than just the product of her imagination?

Sophia couldn't stand the thought of her daughter being caught in this web of darkness. She had to protect Lily. But how? What could she do against something so ancient, so powerful?

Sophia turned toward Lily's bedroom door, a feeling of dread washing over her. She needed answers. She needed to understand what was happening to her daughter before it was too late.

Part Four: Uncovering Hidden Truths

Sophia knew that she couldn't do this alone. She needed help. But who could she turn to? Who could she trust in a situation this bizarre? She couldn't ask the police—they would think she was crazy. She couldn't ask her friends—they would think she was losing her mind. No one would believe her, not until it was too late.

But there was one person she could reach out to—the woman who had been Clara's closest confidante. If anyone knew the truth about Clara's obsession with the door, it was her. Sophia tracked the woman down, an older woman named Margaret Dunn, who now lived in a quiet house on the outskirts of town.

When Sophia arrived at Margaret's home, she was greeted with a warm smile, but Margaret's eyes seemed to betray a deep sadness. She invited Sophia inside, offering tea and a quiet space to talk.

"I'm sorry to bring up old memories," Sophia began, "but I need to understand. What happened to Clara? What was this door she became obsessed with? What did it do to her?"

Margaret's expression shifted, her eyes flickering with a mixture of fear and sorrow. She paused before speaking, as if weighing the decision to share the truth.

"She was never the same after she started drawing the door," Margaret said softly, her voice trembling slightly. "At first, it was just sketches—simple things. But then... it changed her. The door, it wasn't just a picture. It was something real. Something alive."

Sophia leaned forward, her heart pounding. "What do you mean? What was it?"

Margaret closed her eyes for a moment, as though recalling something she wished she could forget. "I don't know, but I think Clara opened something—something she shouldn't have. She thought it was a way to find peace, but it wasn't. It was a doorway to something far worse. And once you open it... you can't close it again."

Sophia felt the air leave her lungs. This was exactly what she had feared. Lily was on the same path as Clara, and she didn't know how to stop it.

PART FIVE: THE WARNING Signs

Sophia couldn't shake the nagging feeling that something was closing in on her, that time was running out for Lily. Margaret's words echoed in her mind—"Once you open it, you can't close it again." What did that mean for her daughter? Was there still time to intervene, or had Lily already been touched by whatever dark force had claimed Clara all those years ago?

Sophia returned to the archives and the journals she'd gathered, her fingers moving quickly, scanning page after page. She felt a sense of urgency, an instinct telling her that the truth was within reach. As she sifted through the old photographs of Clara, the memories of her friends, and the reports of her disappearance, she noticed something she hadn't before: a pattern. Clara's descent into obsession had followed a predictable trajectory. At first, the drawings were innocent enough—just lines and swirls, little more than the musings of a young girl with an active imagination. But then, the drawings changed. The door began to take shape, and with it, the symbols. The dark shapes that emerged alongside it were cryptic and disturbing.

The more Clara sketched, the more her behavior had become erratic. She began speaking to herself in a strange, hushed tone, her eyes vacant as if listening to something only she could hear. She would wander the house at night, calling out for someone—"It's not too late. The door is still open." Her friends had tried to intervene, to bring her back from the edge, but they'd failed. Clara had insisted she was fine, that the door was her escape from the pain she carried.

But what had happened to Clara after she disappeared? The authorities had never found any trace of her, but Sophia had uncovered an unsettling rumor that had surfaced in whispers after the investigation had cooled: Clara's body had never been found because Clara had never truly disappeared. She had left. Stepped through the door. And those who had searched for her had come to believe something far more sinister had been at play—that Clara hadn't just vanished, but had become something else. Something lost to the dark.

Sophia's breath caught in her throat. Could this be the same fate that awaited Lily? Could the door be calling her too?

Part Six: Digging Deeper

Determined to find more answers, Sophia sought out the local library, where she knew the missing person's case on Clara Bennett was still archived in the basement. As she made her way into the dimly lit, dusty corner of the library, she could feel the oppressive weight of the case pressing down on her. The air seemed heavier here, as though the very walls were holding secrets that had been buried for far too long.

Sophia felt a chill run down her spine as she pulled open the file. She had already reviewed the police reports, but this was different. This was the firsthand accounts from those who had known Clara best. The case was more than just a disappearance; it was an open wound in the town's history, one that no one had been able to heal.

She began reading the interviews with Clara's closest friends, and the deeper she went, the more horrified she became. Several people described Clara in her final days as though she were in a trance, as if something or someone had taken control of her mind. It wasn't just the door anymore—there were whispers of something far darker: **visions**. Clara had claimed that the door was a passage to another world, one that had promised to give her the answers she had been seeking all her life. But with each day that passed, Clara grew more convinced that she was meant to be a part of this other world.

Sophia felt a tightening in her chest. She needed to know more about what this "other world" was. The phrase echoed in her mind—"The Other Side." What if Clara's fate wasn't a one-time occurrence? What if Lily was destined for the same path?

She continued reading, a sense of dread growing as she discovered that several other people in town had begun to have dreams and visions of the door. They spoke of it with unease, as if it was something that called to them in the dead of night. But no one had ever dared to go near it. Clara had been the only one brave—or perhaps desperate—enough to try. The library's files hinted at a strange, hidden history surrounding the door, one that reached further back than Clara's time—an ancient secret tied to the town itself.

Part Seven: A Frightening Revelation

Sophia spent the next few days obsessively reviewing every piece of information she had gathered. She couldn't stop thinking about one particular detail in Clara's last diary entry. The words stood out like a flashing red warning light: *"I can't escape. I'm afraid of what will happen when I step through. But I have to go."*

What had Clara known? And why had she been so convinced that she needed to go through the door?

As Sophia contemplated these questions, she received an unexpected phone call. It was Margaret Dunn, the woman she had spoken to earlier, the one who had shared what little she knew about Clara's obsession. Margaret's voice was shaky when she spoke.

"You need to be careful, Sophia," she said, her words strained. "The door is not something you can control. If Lily is starting to see it... hear it... then it's already too late. You can't protect her from it."

Sophia's mind reeled. What did Margaret mean? How could it already be too late? Was there something she hadn't told her?

"I—what do you mean?" Sophia's voice wavered with panic. "What happens once she's drawn to it? What will it do to her?"

Margaret's voice was barely a whisper. "It takes them. It doesn't give them back."

Sophia's blood ran cold. She had feared something like this, but hearing it confirmed made her stomach churn. The door wasn't just a passage—it was a trap. And if Lily had already been marked by it, there might be no way to stop the pull.

Sophia felt the room closing in around her, her pulse racing. She had to act fast. She couldn't let history repeat itself. She needed to protect Lily. But how could she fight something she didn't fully understand?

Part Eight: Descent into Madness

The days that followed were filled with a constant sense of dread. Sophia's every instinct told her to get Lily away from the house, to take her somewhere far, far away from the door. But she couldn't. It was already too late for that. Lily was already slipping further and further away, her behavior becoming more erratic, her drawings more disturbing. The whispers of the door seemed to follow her wherever she went.

Sophia tried to reach out to Lily, to get through to her, but it felt as though her daughter were slipping through her fingers, becoming something she didn't recognize. The bond they had once shared, the unspoken connection between mother and child, was fraying at the edges, and Sophia had no idea how to mend it.

One night, as Sophia was about to tuck Lily into bed, she found her daughter sitting on the floor, staring at the wall. Her back was to Sophia, but Sophia could feel the shift in the atmosphere. Something was different—something had changed in her daughter.

"What's wrong, Lily?" Sophia asked softly, kneeling beside her.

Lily didn't respond. She just sat there, her eyes wide and glassy, as if she were looking at something Sophia couldn't see. Slowly, Lily turned her head, her gaze locking onto her mother's. Her voice, when she spoke, was hollow, devoid of emotion.

"I see it, Mom," Lily whispered. "I see the door. It's waiting for me."

Sophia's heart shattered as she held Lily close, but deep inside, she felt the overwhelming pull of the truth. Whatever force had claimed Clara Bennett, it was coming for her daughter too.

Part Nine: Unveiling the Past

The following week, Sophia could no longer ignore the overwhelming weight of the truth that pressed against her chest. Every day, as she watched Lily struggle more with her cryptic drawings and unsettling behavior, the connection between her daughter and Clara Bennett became undeniable. But it was more than just a familial resemblance—there was something ancient and sinister about the entire situation, something the town had buried deep within its history.

Sophia found herself standing in front of the old town hall one afternoon, staring at the weathered building. It was time to speak to someone who had known Clara better than anyone else. And there was one person in town who might have more information—Clara's childhood friend, James Holloway.

James had been a quiet, unassuming man who had never left the town. He had grown up with Clara, and it was rumored that they had been close, possibly more than just friends. But after Clara disappeared, James had become reclusive, retreating into a life of solitude. He rarely left his house on the outskirts of town, and when he did, it was only to buy food from the local market. Sophia had tried calling him several times in the past few weeks, but he refused to answer.

Now, with the urgency mounting and Lily's behavior becoming more erratic by the day, Sophia knew she had no choice but to confront him face to face.

Part Ten: The Unwilling Confidant

The small cottage James lived in was nestled at the edge of a forest, surrounded by overgrown foliage. The air seemed thicker here, as if the trees were closing in, sheltering the secrets that James had kept for years. As Sophia walked up the cracked stone path to the front door, her heart raced with anticipation. She knocked three times, each tap louder than the last.

After a few moments, the door creaked open, revealing James. His face was weathered, and his eyes were weary, as though he hadn't slept in years. There was a sadness in his gaze that immediately made Sophia uneasy. He didn't speak at first, just stood there, his eyes lingering on her with suspicion.

"I need to talk to you about Clara," Sophia said softly, trying to keep her voice steady. "I'm trying to understand what happened to her."

James stiffened, his face paling slightly. He stepped back, allowing her to enter, but his movements were slow, cautious. The interior of the cottage was cluttered with old books, papers, and strange artifacts, the air thick with the smell of mildew and dust. It looked as though time had stopped inside this place, just as it had for James after Clara's disappearance.

"I've already told the police everything I know," he said gruffly, sitting down in a worn-out armchair by the fireplace.

Sophia took a seat across from him, her eyes scanning the room. The shelves were filled with books on mysticism, occult symbols, and folklore. Some of them looked ancient, their pages yellowed with age. Her eyes were drawn to a particularly old leather-bound tome that sat on the table in front of James. It was open, revealing a page with intricate sketches of doors—symbols that matched the ones in Clara's last journal entry.

"Clara didn't just disappear," James began, his voice cracking. "She wasn't... taken. She chose it. She chose to go through the door."

Sophia's heart skipped a beat. "What do you mean? What door?"

James closed his eyes, as if gathering his strength. When he opened them again, they were filled with a haunting knowledge that Sophia could barely comprehend. "There's a legend. One that's been passed down for generations. The door isn't just a doorway—it's a portal. A doorway to another world, another dimension. But it's not just any world. It's a place of darkness, a place that takes what it wants."

Sophia leaned forward, her pulse quickening. "And Clara... she went there willingly?"

James nodded, the weight of the memory bearing down on him. "She didn't understand what she was doing. She thought she was escaping, that she was finally going to find the answers to all the questions she had about her life. But the door doesn't give answers. It takes. It takes your soul, your essence... and once you cross through, there's no going back."

Sophia felt the blood drain from her face. "And you think Lily is going to do the same thing?"

James hesitated, glancing away. "Lily... she's already marked. I'm sorry to say it, but it's true. The same thing that happened to Clara is happening to her. The drawings, the visions, the whispers—she's already been touched by it."

Sophia's mind reeled. "But why her? Why Clara, and why now Lily?"

James's face twisted with pain, his voice barely a whisper. "The door doesn't choose randomly. It's connected to the town's history—this place has always been cursed. And every generation, it calls to someone. Clara was the last one to answer, but Lily—she's the one it's been waiting for."

Part Eleven: The Curse of the Door

Sophia felt as if the world had just tilted beneath her feet. Her mind was spinning with the impossible truth that James had just laid before her. The door was not just a metaphor or a figment of Clara's imagination—it was real, and it was part of something much larger, something older than the town itself.

"This door—where is it?" Sophia asked, her voice trembling.

James's eyes flickered with uncertainty, but he nodded toward the window that faced the forest. "The entrance is hidden. It's not far from here, deep in the woods. Only a few people know where it is. It's been kept secret, locked away. But once it calls to you, there's no way to shut it again."

Sophia's thoughts were a blur. She had to get to the door. She had to stop this from happening to Lily, to save her from the same fate that had claimed Clara. But how? And what would she find if she followed the trail into the woods?

Before she could speak, James looked at her one last time, his face filled with regret and sorrow. "Be careful, Sophia. If you go after her, you may never return. The door doesn't just take—sometimes, it leaves something else behind. And I don't know if you'll be able to save her."

Sophia's heart pounded in her chest. There was no turning back now. She had to go, even if it meant risking everything to save Lily.

Chapter Four: Echoes of Danger

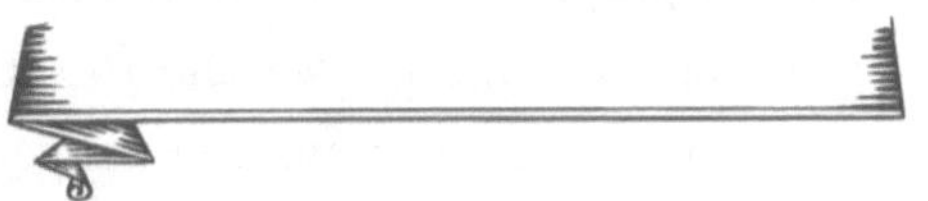

Sophia didn't sleep that night. The events of the past few days—the chilling conversation with James, the new knowledge of the door, and the unsettling behavior of Lily—rattled her to the core. She had always believed that her town, its history, and its people were grounded in normalcy, even if there had been a few whispered legends over the years. But now, the veil had been lifted, and the sinister truth was clear. Her daughter was in danger. The door, the very thing that had claimed Clara Bennett, was calling to Lily, and there was no telling what consequences awaited them if she didn't act soon.

With the weight of the knowledge pressing heavily on her chest, Sophia felt an overwhelming need to find the door. She had no idea what she would encounter once she reached it, but the stakes had become too high to turn back. It was a race against time, and she had to be ready for whatever lay ahead.

She could still hear James's voice echoing in her mind: *The door doesn't just take—sometimes, it leaves something else behind.* The warning haunted her thoughts as she paced around her house, trying to make sense of everything. The woods, the portal, the curse—it was all too much, too overwhelming. Yet, in her gut, she knew one thing for certain: she had to protect Lily at all costs.

PART ONE: INTO THE Darkness

The morning light crept into Sophia's living room, casting long shadows across the floor. She felt the pull to go, to find the truth before it swallowed them whole. After packing a small bag with essentials—flashlight, water, her phone, and a first-aid kit—Sophia dressed in dark clothes, prepared for the hike into the woods. She couldn't afford to be caught unprepared; the forest held too many secrets, and she needed to be ready for whatever dangers it might throw her way.

Lily had been quiet all morning, staring at her drawings in silence. She hadn't uttered a word, but Sophia could see the confusion in her eyes, the growing dread. Something was happening to her, and Sophia could see the toll it was taking on her spirit. Sophia had no illusions—Lily wasn't just acting strange; she was being pulled toward something darker, something ancient. And the longer they stayed in town, the more the pull grew.

Sophia kissed Lily's forehead before leaving. "I'll be back soon, sweetheart. I just need to take care of something."

Lily didn't respond, just looked at her with wide, uncertain eyes. For the first time, Sophia realized her daughter was afraid of her own future. But Sophia had no choice. She couldn't let Lily walk down a path from which there would be no return.

As she walked toward the forest's edge, the air grew heavy, thick with an unnatural stillness. The trees, dense and old, seemed to lean in, as if they knew she was trespassing on forbidden ground. The faint sound of birds was absent, leaving only the sound of her boots crunching on the dry leaves beneath her feet.

Sophia had always known there was something unsettling about the woods—the way they seemed to stretch on forever, the sense of isolation they held. But today, that feeling of unease was sharper than ever. The deeper she ventured, the more she could sense an oppressive force, an invisible weight that clung to her every step.

Part Two: The Web of Secrets

She had spent the better part of the day trekking through the forest. The sky above had dimmed to a muted gray, casting shadows that seemed to writhe and twist. It wasn't until dusk that she came across something unusual: a stone structure, half-buried under a blanket of ivy and moss. At first, it looked like a ruin, perhaps the remnants of an old foundation. But as she drew closer, she realized it was a door.

A large, arching stone doorway, its shape weathered by time, loomed before her. The structure seemed out of place, as if it didn't belong among the towering trees or the untamed wilderness. The door itself was ornate, its carvings intricate, almost otherworldly. Symbols—symbols she had seen before in Clara Bennett's drawings—were etched into the stone, creating an eerie glow in the fading light.

Sophia's breath caught in her throat as she reached out, her hand trembling as it brushed against the stone. The air around her crackled with a strange energy, and for a split second, she felt as if the forest itself was holding its breath. It was here. The door that James had warned her about. The door that could either save Lily—or destroy her.

With a deep breath, Sophia stepped closer. Her heart pounded in her chest, her mind spinning with a thousand questions. What was this place? What had happened to Clara, and what did it have to do with Lily?

As her hand hovered over the door's surface, she felt a sudden pull—a tug deep inside her, as though the door itself was calling to her. She jerked her hand back, her pulse racing. Her body screamed for her to run, to leave this place, but her mind refused. She couldn't abandon her daughter. Not now. Not when the answers were so close.

Suddenly, a voice broke the silence, so soft and distant it was barely audible.

"She's coming…"

Sophia whipped around, searching the shadows for the source of the voice. Her eyes scanned the trees, her breath quickening as she strained to hear more, but there was only the whispering wind.

She's coming... The voice seemed to reverberate inside her head, carrying with it an undeniable sense of urgency. Whoever—*whatever*—spoke those words knew exactly what was at stake. And in that moment, Sophia knew she was running out of time.

Part Three: Buried Threats

The forest seemed to shift around her, its once familiar paths now a maze of unfamiliarity. Sophia's mind was filled with conflicting thoughts—her responsibility to her daughter, the chilling warnings from James, and the undeniable sense that the door was not just a passageway, but something far more insidious.

As she made her way back toward the edge of the forest, the shadows grew longer, and the sense of foreboding intensified. She could feel the weight of eyes upon her, as if the woods themselves were watching, waiting for her to make the next move.

She wasn't alone.

Sophia quickened her pace, heart hammering in her chest. The danger she had been running from had caught up to her. The door wasn't just a doorway—it was a trap, a mechanism set into motion by an unseen hand. And now, the town's buried secrets were rising to the surface, threatening to consume everything in their path.

Part Four: The Web Unraveling

Back at her house, Sophia was no closer to understanding the full extent of what she had uncovered. The door, the whispers, the growing sense of malevolent power—they were all connected in ways she could scarcely comprehend. She sat at her kitchen table, sifting through Clara Bennett's journal and old newspaper clippings, trying to make sense of the fragments.

The deeper she dug into Clara's past, the more she realized how deeply intertwined it was with the town's own dark history. A pattern began to emerge—one that tied Clara, Lily, and the door to a long-forgotten pact, a secret kept by the town's founders. The echoes of danger had existed long before Sophia had ever arrived here, and they would continue long after she was gone.

The question now was: *What could she do to stop it?*

Sophia knew she was standing on the precipice of something far greater than herself. The web of secrets that had held this town in its grip for generations was unraveling, and she was at its center. The clock was ticking. If she didn't act soon, everything—her daughter's life, the town, and perhaps even her own—would be lost.

Sophia sat motionless at the kitchen table, Clara Bennett's journal open in front of her. The words blurred before her eyes, her thoughts scattered as the pieces of the puzzle began to connect in troubling ways. The whispers, the door, the cryptic references to "the others" and "the gateway" in Clara's journal—they were all part of something much bigger than anything Sophia had anticipated. The door wasn't just an anomaly, a relic of the past; it was a living, breathing entity, an anchor to something beyond their world.

As the weight of the discovery settled over her, Sophia's mind raced through the threads of Clara's writings. Clara had known something. The woman had left behind warnings and cryptic symbols—warnings about the price one must pay to open the door. And the most disturbing entry of all was the one that mentioned Lily.

"She is the key. The one they will take, the one they need. The door calls to her as it called to me."

Sophia's hands trembled as she turned the page. *The door calls to her.* It wasn't a coincidence. Lily had been drawing those strange, cryptic symbols without understanding their meaning. She had been speaking of things from the past, things she couldn't possibly know. Sophia felt a deep, irrational fear surge in her chest. *Was Lily the key? Was she meant to open the door, just as Clara had been?*

Sophia forced herself to push the journal aside, shaking her head as though to rid herself of the thoughts. But they clung to her like shadows, seeping into her every thought. The door wasn't just a physical structure hidden in the woods—it was an anchor to something far more sinister. A doorway to another world. A place that no one should ever visit. And now, her daughter was caught in its grasp.

She had to act. There was no time to waste.

Part Five: A Web of Hidden Threats

The next morning, Sophia did not waste any time. She had to figure out how to protect Lily. The door had already begun to call to her daughter, and every minute they wasted was a minute closer to disaster. She had to find a way to close it, to sever whatever connection had formed between Lily and the entity behind the door.

Sophia's first instinct was to find James again. He knew more than he had let on. She could sense it. There was an urgency in his eyes, something he hadn't fully shared with her. Perhaps now he would be more willing to help, now that she knew the gravity of the situation.

She drove to the bar where James worked, her thoughts racing with questions she couldn't even begin to articulate. When she entered, she found James behind the bar, polishing glasses. His eyes met hers immediately, and for a moment, they just stood there, exchanging a look full of unspoken understanding. He must have known what she had uncovered.

"You've been to the door," James said, his voice low. He didn't ask. It wasn't a question—it was a statement.

Sophia nodded, the weight of her actions pressing down on her. "I found it. The door. It's real."

James sighed, setting the glass down with a soft clink. "I should've known you'd go looking for it. You don't give up easily."

Sophia felt her anger flare at his casual response. "You knew about this, didn't you? You knew what it could do. You didn't warn me. You let me bring Lily here. Do you have any idea what's happening to her?"

James leaned forward, his face serious. "I didn't think you were ready. Hell, I didn't think anyone would believe it. But you're right—it's happening. The door is opening again, and Lily... she's connected to it, whether we want her to be or not."

Sophia's heart dropped. "What do you mean, connected?"

James ran a hand through his hair, looking conflicted. "The door doesn't just open and close. It's alive. And when it calls, it's looking for something. A vessel, a conduit. Clara—she was the first, but she wasn't the last. The door picks people. And now, it's picked Lily."

Sophia's breath caught in her throat. "What can we do to stop it?"

James's eyes darkened. "There are ways to close it. But they're dangerous. You have to be willing to make a sacrifice."

Sophia clenched her fists, her heart racing. "I'll do whatever it takes. Tell me what to do."

He nodded, but there was hesitation in his voice. "You have to understand something. The door doesn't just want someone to open it—it's looking for something to stay. If you close it without understanding the cost, it will try to claim another."

Sophia felt her pulse quicken as the weight of his words settled in. "What does that mean for Lily? Will she—will she be taken?"

James looked away, unable to meet her eyes. "If she's the one who's meant to stay... it might already be too late."

Sophia's stomach turned, and she felt sick. "So there's no way to stop it?"

James shook his head, his expression grim. "There's always a way. But it comes with a price. You have to be ready to give up everything, even if it means losing the one you love."

The room seemed to close in on her, the walls pressing against her as the weight of the decision settled upon her. Lily's safety came first, but at what cost? Sophia had never been one to back down from a challenge, but this—this was different. This wasn't just a fight against time; it was a fight against something that existed outside the boundaries of her understanding.

"Tell me what to do," she whispered, her voice filled with a quiet desperation.

James met her gaze, his eyes filled with regret. "You have to face the door. Face what's inside. And you can only close it if you understand the full truth of what it is. The thing is... the truth isn't something anyone can live with."

Sophia's heart pounded in her chest. She had already made up her mind. She had no choice. For Lily, for her family, she would face the darkness. But she knew deep down that whatever she was about to discover could change everything. The door wasn't just a portal—it was a gateway to something far more dangerous. And whatever secrets it held, Sophia was determined to uncover them, no matter the cost.

Part Six: Confronting the Past

That evening, Sophia stood at the edge of the forest once again, staring at the ancient stone doorway. The air was heavy, the forest silent in its unnerving stillness. She had come to find answers, but now, standing before the door, she wasn't sure if she was ready to face what lay behind it.

The wind whispered through the trees, carrying with it a sense of urgency. The door wasn't just a physical barrier—it was a force, a power that had been waiting for her. And now that she was here, she could feel the pull, the magnetic force that seemed to draw her in.

She placed a trembling hand against the cold stone, and for the first time, she felt something shift beneath her skin. The ground seemed to tremble, and the whispers from earlier returned, louder now, swirling around her like an ominous storm.

"She's coming... she's the one."

The voice echoed inside her mind, a cold, malevolent whisper that sent shivers down her spine. Sophia took a deep breath and stepped forward, determined to uncover the truth, no matter the cost.

Chapter Five: Dreams of the Forgotten

Lily's dreams had always been vivid. But lately, they had become more intense, more real, as if they were pieces of a puzzle she couldn't quite put together. Every morning, she woke up with the lingering feeling of something just out of reach—something important. Sophia had noticed the change. Her daughter, once a cheerful and talkative little girl, had grown more distant, her eyes often vacant, as though she were lost in a world only she could see.

It was the dreams. Sophia had no doubt of it.

The first night Lily had mentioned them, she simply said, "I saw a lady, Mommy. She was sad, but she smiled at me."

Sophia had chalked it up to the child's imagination, a product of an overactive mind before bedtime. But then the dreams became more frequent, and the stories more elaborate.

On one occasion, Lily had woken in the middle of the night, trembling. Sophia rushed to her side, her heart pounding with worry. "Lily? What's wrong?"

Her daughter had clutched the blanket, her small body trembling as she whispered, "I dreamt I was in a place, Mommy. It was dark, and the walls were cold and wet. There was a woman, but she wasn't happy. She looked like she wanted to say something, but no sound came out."

Sophia's breath caught in her throat. The description, while vague, triggered something deep in her. She couldn't explain it, but the feeling gnawed at her, like a memory just out of reach. "What do you mean? What was the woman doing?"

Lily's voice had quivered. "She was standing by a door. A big, dark door, and she kept pointing at it. But when I tried to go through it, the door wouldn't open."

Sophia tucked her daughter back into bed, her mind racing. The recurring details—dark places, doors, women—were unsettling. And as the nights passed, the dreams became even more specific. Each time Lily awoke, there was a new piece of the puzzle.

Lily's eyes were wide as she spoke one morning, a haunted look in her eyes. "Mommy, she said my name. The lady. She said 'Lily, you're the one.'"

Sophia had frozen in place, her heart sinking into her stomach. What did that mean? Was her daughter speaking of Clara? The woman whose disappearance had haunted Sophia for years?

She had asked Lily, gently, "Do you know who the lady is, sweetie?"

Lily shook her head. "No. But I think she's important. I think she's waiting for me."

Sophia felt a chill sweep through her, an unsettling feeling creeping over her like an unwanted shadow. She had heard the rumors, the stories about Clara Bennett, the woman who had vanished without a trace all those years ago. But the more she tried to push those thoughts from her mind, the more the pieces of the puzzle seemed to fit together. Could Lily somehow be connected to Clara? And if so, why?

The dreams continued, each one more vivid than the last. One night, Lily had told her about standing in front of a beautiful house, a house she described as "old and full of secrets." Inside, she said, there was a room filled with mirrors. "I couldn't see my reflection," she whispered, "but I could feel something behind me. Watching me."

Sophia had immediately thought of Clara's disappearance. The mirrors. The idea of being watched. It was all too much of a coincidence. She had to know more.

Lily's dreams began to bleed into her waking life, the lines between the two worlds blurring. During the day, she would sometimes stare at the walls, her gaze distant and unfocused. Her hands would tremble, her eyes wide with confusion as if she were seeing something no one else could.

"I'm not crazy, Mommy," Lily had said one day, her voice small but insistent. "I can see her. The lady. She's in my dreams, but she's here too."

Sophia had sat beside her daughter, her mind whirling. There had to be something connecting these dreams, something that tied Lily to Clara Bennett. But what? And why now?

The answers were elusive, like wisps of smoke slipping through her fingers. But one thing was becoming clearer: these dreams weren't just figments of Lily's imagination. They were clues. Pieces of a forgotten story that Sophia had to unravel before it was too late.

Sophia couldn't ignore it anymore. The feeling in her gut told her that the answers lay hidden in the past, in the life of Clara Bennett. But what could the connection between a missing woman and her daughter mean? And how far back did it go?

Late one night, after Lily had fallen into a restless sleep, Sophia sat in the dim light of the kitchen, her fingers brushing the edges of the old newspaper clippings she had found. The articles about Clara's disappearance, the rumors of paranormal activity surrounding her last known location, the unexplained events that had occurred in the wake of her vanishing. They were all linked—each one leading Sophia closer to an answer she wasn't sure she was ready to find.

As she stared at the articles, something caught her eye. A small detail buried in the corner of one article: a mention of an old house—Clara's childhood home. Sophia's breath caught in her throat. It was the same house Lily had described in her dream. The old, forgotten house.

The pieces were finally starting to fit together, but with each new discovery, the questions multiplied. Who was the lady in Lily's dreams? What was she trying to communicate? And what did all of this have to do with Clara's disappearance?

Sophia couldn't ignore the gnawing feeling in her gut. She had to find the house. She had to understand what connection it had to Clara and why Lily was being drawn into a web of memories and ghosts from the past.

But with each passing day, Sophia felt like she was getting closer to something much darker, something far more dangerous than she had ever imagined.

The dreams weren't just dreams. They were memories. But whose? And were they truly Lily's—or had they been planted in her mind by something far more sinister?

Sophia stood up, her decision made. She would find the house. She would uncover the truth. Whatever it took.

And if the ghosts of the past were waiting for her, she would face them head-on, for Lily's sake.

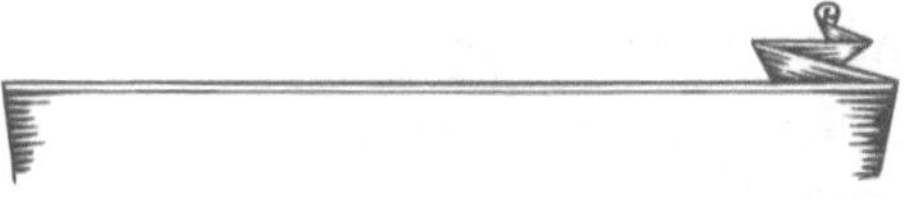

Chapter Six: The Puzzle Piece

The house felt like a mausoleum. Even in the weak light filtering through the rotting windowpanes, every inch of the place seemed to be weighed down with years of neglect, sadness, and untold secrets. Sophia's heart pounded in her chest as she walked deeper into the crumbling structure. Her fingers brushed against the peeling wallpaper, the faded remnants of a time long gone. There was a heavy sense of foreboding that hung in the air, like a warning sign telling her to turn back, yet she pressed forward.

The house had been silent, but now, in this eerie stillness, every sound felt amplified—the faint creak of the floorboards beneath her feet, the distant rustling of wind against the broken windows, the rhythmic ticking of an old, abandoned clock in the corner. Every corner of the house seemed to be a piece of a long-forgotten puzzle, its secrets lying in wait to be uncovered. But Sophia knew that each step she took only made the mystery more complex, more dangerous.

She couldn't shake the feeling that this place was the key. Her pulse quickened as her thoughts raced. *This is where it all began.* She wasn't just uncovering Clara Bennett's past anymore—she was learning something that tied her own daughter to this house, this tragic history. Sophia's steps grew more deliberate as she made her way to the basement door. It was the door Lily had described to her in detail, the one that had haunted her dreams for weeks. The one that seemed to be pulling Sophia into its depths.

The basement door creaked open with a groan, revealing a dark, narrow staircase. Her stomach churned with unease as she descended, the air growing colder with each step. The flickering light from her phone's flashlight revealed the musty, damp walls of the basement. The faint smell of mildew and decay filled the air, and her breath caught in her throat as she reached the bottom.

The basement was cluttered with old furniture, stacks of newspapers, and boxes of forgotten belongings. But it wasn't the debris that caught her attention—it was something else. A large, ornate chest sat in the corner, its wooden surface covered in layers of dust. The chest looked old—ancient, even. Sophia couldn't explain it, but she was drawn to it, as if something deep within her was telling her that it was important. Something had been hidden there, and it was time for her to find it.

She approached cautiously, her fingers trembling as she reached out to open the chest. The lid creaked as it lifted, revealing a collection of items that seemed utterly out of place. Old photographs, a few pieces of clothing, and several faded letters—things that didn't belong to Clara Bennett but felt strangely familiar. One photograph in particular stood out. It was an old black-and-white image of a family, the faces ghostly and worn with age. Sophia squinted at the photograph, but it was the figure in the back row that captured her attention. A woman with long, dark hair. She was smiling, but there was something about her expression—something in her eyes—that sent a chill running down Sophia's spine.

Is this Clara? Sophia's thoughts raced, but a voice deep inside her told her that it wasn't Clara's face she was looking at—it was someone else's.

Then, hidden beneath the photograph, Sophia found a small, leather-bound notebook. She opened it, flipping through the yellowed pages, each filled with hastily scrawled handwriting. The words were barely legible, but Sophia could make out enough to know that these were Clara's thoughts, her reflections on the events leading up to her disappearance. As Sophia read, she realized the disturbing truth: Clara had been documenting something far darker than a simple family tragedy. These were not just memories—these were warnings.

Sophia's hands shook as she read the words aloud, her voice barely above a whisper. *"I know what happened to my parents. I know who's responsible. And they won't stop until they get what they want."*

A wave of nausea washed over Sophia as she closed the book, her mind reeling. She had come here seeking answers, but what she had found was only more questions. Who had Clara been afraid of? And why had she been trying to protect herself—or someone else—by keeping these secrets hidden?

Suddenly, a noise echoed from behind her. Sophia froze, her heart hammering in her chest. She turned, expecting to see Lily standing there, but the basement was empty. The silence stretched on, broken only by the muffled sound of the wind outside. And then she saw it—another photograph, half-hidden beneath a stack of old newspapers.

This time, the photograph was different. It wasn't a family photo. It wasn't even a picture of Clara. It was a faded image of a man, his face obscured by shadows, but his posture unmistakable. Sophia stared at it, her breath catching in her throat. The figure in the photograph was unmistakable—*it was someone she knew.*

Sophia sat in stunned silence, clutching the photograph in her hands. The man in the picture was someone from her past, someone she had known years ago, before Lily had been born. His name was Ryan, and he had been a brief but significant part of her life. But the memories of him were hazy—there had been too much time, too many years, for her to fully remember the details. She had never imagined that his name would resurface in this way, tied to a mystery that had nothing to do with her own life—yet everything to do with Lily.

As the truth began to sink in, Sophia realized that Ryan had been connected to Clara, and by extension, to Lily. *Had he been a part of Clara's life?* she wondered. And more chillingly, *was he somehow involved in the events that led to Clara's disappearance?*

Her mind raced as she sifted through the fragments of memory she had of Ryan. He had always been enigmatic, elusive in a way that made Sophia feel uneasy even when they had shared a brief but intense connection. It wasn't until much later that she had learned of his troubled past, his connection to some of the darker corners of society. And yet, she had never once thought that he could have been involved in the tragedy that surrounded Clara.

But the evidence was becoming undeniable. Ryan's name, his image, his presence in Clara's life—it was all coming together in a way that made Sophia's skin crawl. He had been a part of the puzzle, a piece that had been hidden for far too long.

Sophia knew that there was no turning back now. She had to confront this head-on, no matter where it led. If Ryan was involved in Clara's disappearance, then Lily was in grave danger. The puzzle pieces were coming together, but they were only revealing a more terrifying picture.

Sophia locked the chest and left the basement, her mind in turmoil. She knew she had to act quickly, but every step she took seemed to bring her closer to an inevitable confrontation. She didn't know who to trust, and she wasn't sure if she could trust herself. But one thing was certain: the deeper she dug, the more dangerous it became. The secrets she was uncovering were darker than she could have ever imagined, and if she wasn't careful, she might find herself caught in a web of lies and deceit that was impossible to escape.

Lily, she realized, was the key to everything. Her daughter had been having the dreams, seeing the images of the house, the photographs, the dark figures. Somehow, she was connected to it all. And now, more than ever, Sophia needed to understand why. She needed to protect her daughter from the danger that lurked just beneath the surface.

But first, she had to confront the man in the photograph. And that meant going back to the beginning. Back to Ryan.

Chapter Seven: The Unraveling

Section One: A Quiet Warning

Sophia Reed sat at her kitchen table, bathed in the faint glow of a single overhead light. The house was unusually quiet, save for the ticking of the clock on the wall. It was the kind of stillness that brought with it a sense of foreboding. Her laptop screen displayed a collection of scanned notes, newspaper clippings, and Lily's drawings, all spread out before her like a puzzle waiting to be solved. Each piece hinted at Clara Bennett's mysterious disappearance, yet none fit neatly together.

Her phone buzzed sharply, slicing through the silence. Sophia jumped slightly, her hand knocking over a mug of tea. Cursing under her breath, she wiped the spill and grabbed the phone. The screen displayed an unknown number.

She hesitated, her thumb hovering over the screen. These days, every call, every interaction seemed fraught with potential danger. With a deep breath, she answered.

"Hello?"

A brief pause followed, filled with static. Then a distorted voice crackled through.

"Stop digging, Ms. Reed. You don't know what you're getting into."

Sophia's grip on the phone tightened. "Who is this?"

The voice ignored her question. "For your sake—and your daughter's—drop this now."

The line went dead.

Sophia's pulse raced as she stared at the phone. Her first instinct was to call the police, but she quickly dismissed the idea. What would she even report? An anonymous threat from a blocked number? That wouldn't help. She stood abruptly, pacing the kitchen as her mind raced.

Her thoughts turned to Lily, who was upstairs asleep—or at least she hoped so. Recently, Lily's nights had been anything but restful, plagued by vivid dreams and sleeptalking episodes that left her visibly drained. Sophia hurried up the stairs, her feet barely making a sound on the carpeted steps.

She peeked into Lily's room. The soft glow of a nightlight illuminated the space, casting shadows on the walls. Lily lay curled up under her blanket, her small frame rising and falling with each breath. Sophia lingered for a moment, letting the sight of her daughter bring a fleeting sense of calm.

Returning to her bedroom, she double-checked the locks on the windows and doors. The strange call had rattled her, but she was no stranger to fear. It had been her constant companion since the day Lily first uttered Clara Bennett's name.

A GROWING UNEASE

The following morning, Sophia awoke to find Lily sitting at the kitchen table, scribbling furiously in her sketchbook. Her breakfast sat untouched.

"Morning, sweetheart," Sophia said cautiously, pouring herself a cup of coffee.

Lily didn't look up. Her pencil moved with precise, almost mechanical strokes.

Sophia set her mug down and leaned over to see what her daughter was drawing. It was a sprawling landscape, one that Sophia didn't recognize. At its center was a dilapidated cabin surrounded by dense trees. The detail was astonishing—shadows played across the wooden beams of the cabin, and the forest seemed almost alive with texture and depth.

"Lily, what is this?"

Lily finally looked up, her expression distant. "I don't know. It just came to me."

Sophia frowned. "Have you seen this place before?"

Lily shook her head. "I don't think so. But it feels... familiar."

The unease that had settled in Sophia the previous night returned with force.

"Finish your breakfast," she said, trying to sound lighthearted. "We'll talk more about it later."

A Mysterious Trespasser

That afternoon, Sophia decided to step out for groceries. She hesitated to leave Lily alone, but her daughter insisted she would be fine. As a precaution, Sophia set up a basic security camera in the living room, one she could monitor from her phone.

When she returned an hour later, she found Lily sitting on the couch, her sketchbook open in her lap. She was eerily calm, her expression unreadable.

"Everything okay?" Sophia asked, placing the bags on the counter.

Lily nodded, but something in her demeanor made Sophia uneasy. She checked the security footage on her phone. Most of the clips showed Lily quietly drawing, but one segment caught her attention.

A figure appeared briefly on the porch, lingering near the front door. The person wore a dark hoodie, the brim pulled low to obscure their face. After a few seconds, they turned and walked away.

Sophia's heart raced as she replayed the footage. She hadn't noticed anything amiss when she arrived home, but now the idea that someone had been so close—and possibly watching Lily—filled her with dread.

SOPHIA'S RESOLVE

That night, Sophia installed additional locks on the doors and windows. She also placed a chair under the doorknob of the front door, an old habit from her college days.

Lily watched silently as her mother moved around the house.

"Mom, are we in danger?" she asked finally.

Sophia paused, kneeling in front of her daughter. "I won't let anything happen to you, Lily. I promise."

"But the dreams," Lily whispered. "They're not just dreams, are they?"

Sophia didn't know how to answer. How could she explain to her daughter that she wasn't sure of anything anymore? That the world they lived in had become a maze of secrets and shadows?

Instead, she hugged Lily tightly, wishing she could shield her from whatever storm was coming.

A Midnight Revelation

Sophia woke in the middle of the night to the sound of faint whispers. Groggy and disoriented, she sat up and strained to listen. The whispers grew louder, and she realized they were coming from Lily's room.

She rushed to her daughter's side, finding Lily sitting upright in bed, her eyes wide open but unseeing.

"Lily!" Sophia shook her gently.

Lily blinked, snapping out of the trance. "Mom? What's wrong?"

"You were talking in your sleep," Sophia said, her voice trembling.

"What did I say?"

Sophia hesitated. "It sounded like... you were talking to someone named Clara."

Lily's face paled. "I don't remember."

Sophia tucked her daughter back into bed, but sleep didn't come easily for either of them that night.

A Mother's Fear

Over the next few days, the feeling of being watched intensified. Sophia noticed strange cars parked near the house, people lingering too long on the sidewalk. She began carrying pepper spray and kept her phone charged at all times.

Lily, meanwhile, continued to draw. Her sketches became darker, more vivid. One day, she presented Sophia with a drawing of their house engulfed in flames.

"It's just a dream," Lily said when Sophia asked about it. "But it felt real."

Sophia couldn't shake the feeling that the danger was closer than ever.

As the chapter ended, Sophia resolved to double down on her efforts to uncover the truth—no matter the cost.

Section Two: The Silent Pursuer

Sophia could no longer ignore the sense of being hunted. The strange events surrounding her and Lily had escalated from eerie whispers and unsettling dreams to tangible signs that someone—or something—was closing in on them. She decided to take precautions, beginning with a security consultation.

The technician from the local security company arrived the next morning, a burly man named Grant with an easy smile. Despite his casual demeanor, Sophia scrutinized every detail, uneasy about allowing yet another stranger into their space.

"Shouldn't take more than a couple hours," Grant said, unloading equipment from his van.

"Thank you," Sophia replied, her tone clipped.

She stayed close as Grant worked, watching as he installed cameras at strategic points around the house and reinforced the locks.

"I'll set you up with an app," he explained. "You can monitor everything from your phone. If anything triggers the sensors, you'll get an alert immediately."

Sophia nodded, grateful for the added layer of protection but keenly aware it might not be enough.

A Tense Encounter

That evening, after Lily had gone to bed, Sophia settled onto the couch, scrolling through the app's interface. She tested the cameras, ensuring they captured every angle of the property.

As she reviewed the footage, a motion alert popped up on the screen. Her breath caught.

The camera facing the driveway had detected movement. A figure, barely visible in the shadows, stood near the mailbox.

Sophia's pulse raced as she zoomed in. The person was dressed in dark clothing, their features obscured. They lingered for a moment before retreating into the night.

She called the police immediately, but by the time they arrived, the intruder was long gone. The officer on duty, a young woman named Officer Morales, took Sophia's statement.

"Probably just a prowler," Morales said, though her tone was uncertain. "Let us know if it happens again."

Sophia felt no reassurance from the officer's words.

Clues in the Shadows

The next day, Sophia decided to revisit the stack of research materials she had collected about Clara Bennett. She spread them across the dining table, searching for any overlooked detail that might connect Clara's disappearance to their current situation.

One photograph caught her eye. It was an old image of Clara standing in front of a lakeside cabin, the same cabin Lily had drawn days earlier.

Sophia stared at the picture, her mind racing. Could this cabin hold the answers she was seeking?

She decided to dig deeper into the cabin's location. After hours of searching online, she found a record of its ownership: a man named

Thomas Hensley. According to public records, Hensley had died decades ago, and the property had since been abandoned.

A Dangerous Decision

Sophia's curiosity soon gave way to resolve. She had to visit the cabin. Something about it felt pivotal, as though it was the missing piece in a puzzle that had consumed her life.

That evening, she broached the subject with Lily.

"Sweetheart," she began carefully, "do you remember the cabin you drew?"

Lily nodded, her expression cautious.

"I found out where it is," Sophia continued. "I think we need to go there."

Lily's eyes widened. "You think Clara's there?"

Sophia hesitated. "I don't know. But I think it might help us understand what's happening."

Lily looked down at her hands, her small fingers fidgeting with the edge of her shirt. "Okay," she said softly.

Sophia felt a pang of guilt. She hated dragging Lily further into this mystery, but every instinct told her they couldn't turn back now.

The Journey Begins

Early the next morning, Sophia and Lily packed a small bag and set off for the cabin. It was a two-hour drive through winding country roads, the dense forest growing thicker with each passing mile.

Lily was uncharacteristically quiet, staring out the window as the scenery blurred by. Sophia kept glancing at her in the rearview mirror, her heart heavy with worry.

"You okay back there?" she asked.

Lily nodded but didn't say anything.

The GPS directed them to a dirt road that led deeper into the woods. Sophia's grip tightened on the steering wheel as the car jolted over rocks and uneven terrain.

When the cabin finally came into view, Sophia's breath hitched. It was just as Lily had drawn it: weathered and crumbling, surrounded by towering trees that seemed to close in like sentinels.

A Haunting Discovery

Sophia parked the car and stepped out, her every sense on high alert. The air was heavy with the scent of damp earth and pine, the silence broken only by the rustling of leaves in the wind.

"Stay close to me," she instructed Lily.

They approached the cabin cautiously. The wooden door hung ajar, creaking slightly as it swayed. Sophia pushed it open, revealing an interior frozen in time. Dust coated every surface, and cobwebs hung like drapes from the ceiling.

Lily's eyes were wide as she looked around. "It feels... familiar," she whispered.

Sophia didn't respond, too focused on scanning the room for anything that might provide answers.

In the corner of the cabin, she found a trunk. It was old and battered, the metal hinges rusted. With some effort, she pried it open.

Inside were a collection of items: photographs, letters, and a small, leather-bound journal.

Sophia's hands trembled as she picked up the journal. The name "Clara Bennett" was etched on the cover.

The Journal's Secrets

Sophia and Lily sat on the floor of the cabin, the journal resting between them. Sophia hesitated before opening it, as though the act itself would unleash something she couldn't control.

When she finally turned the first page, her breath caught. The handwriting was delicate, looping across the yellowed paper.

The entries were fragmented, filled with references to strange occurrences and an unnamed fear that seemed to plague Clara in her final days.

"I keep seeing her," one entry read. "She looks just like me. How is that possible?"

Sophia's pulse quickened as she read on. The entries painted a picture of a woman unraveling, her life consumed by an inexplicable connection to someone—or something—she couldn't escape.

Lily pointed to one passage. "That's me," she said softly.

Sophia's heart stopped. "What do you mean?"

Lily looked up at her mother, her eyes filled with an unsettling certainty. "I'm the girl Clara kept seeing."

SECTION THREE: THE Connection Deepens

Sophia stared at Lily, her mind struggling to process her daughter's words. The cabin, the journal, the dreams—everything felt like pieces of a puzzle that were suddenly locking into place, yet the image they formed was incomprehensible.

"Lily, what do you mean you're the girl she kept seeing?" Sophia asked, her voice trembling.

"I don't know how to explain it," Lily replied, her gaze fixed on the journal. "I just know. It's like... I remember things, but they're not my memories."

Sophia's instinct was to dismiss it, to write it off as a child's imagination. But after everything they had experienced, denial was no longer an option.

"Let's keep reading," Sophia said, flipping through the journal.

Echoes in the Journal

The entries grew more erratic as Clara's descent into paranoia became evident. She described seeing "a girl with familiar eyes" in her dreams, sometimes in fleeting glimpses during waking hours.

"I know I'm not losing my mind," one entry read. "She's real. She knows things about me no one else could possibly know."

Sophia couldn't shake the eerie similarity to Lily's experiences.

The journal also mentioned a man—Thomas Hensley—who Clara believed held the answers she sought.

"I confronted him," one entry read. "He didn't deny it. He knows who she is, but he won't tell me why."

Sophia's fingers tightened around the book. Thomas Hensley was the original owner of the cabin. Though deceased, his name had surfaced again, pulling them deeper into the mystery.

The Hidden Compartment

As they sifted through the trunk's contents, Lily suddenly pointed to the floor beneath it. "There's something under there," she said.

Sophia moved the trunk aside, revealing a loose floorboard. She pried it open with a nearby crowbar, revealing a small metal box.

Inside were more letters and photographs, but one item stood out: a locket.

Sophia held it up, examining the intricate design. She opened it to find a small photograph of a young Clara on one side and, shockingly, what appeared to be a child who looked exactly like Lily on the other.

Sophia's breath hitched. "This can't be," she whispered.

"I told you," Lily said softly. "It's me."

Unanswered Questions

The discovery of the locket only deepened the enigma. Sophia couldn't deny the uncanny resemblance between the child in the photograph and her daughter.

They spent the rest of the day combing through the remaining letters. Most were written by Clara, addressed to someone cryptically referred to as "M."

In one letter, Clara wrote:

"I can't keep running. If you're reading this, you need to know the truth. It's not just about me—it's about her. She's the key to everything. Please protect her."

Sophia's heart raced as she reread the passage. Who was "M"? And what truth was Clara so desperate to reveal?

The Cabin's Warning

As dusk fell, an eerie stillness settled over the cabin. Sophia and Lily decided to stay the night, too engrossed in their findings to leave.

But as darkness enveloped the forest, the sense of unease grew. Strange noises echoed outside—branches snapping, whispers carried on the wind.

Sophia armed herself with a flashlight and a kitchen knife she had packed in haste. She checked the doors and windows, ensuring they were locked, but her instincts screamed that they were being watched.

Lily sat cross-legged on the floor, clutching the locket. "She's scared," Lily said suddenly.

Sophia froze. "Who's scared?"

"Clara," Lily replied, her voice barely audible.

The Silent Intruder

In the middle of the night, a loud crash jolted Sophia awake. She grabbed the knife and flashlight, her heart pounding as she crept toward the source of the noise.

The front door was ajar, swinging slightly in the wind.

"Lily, stay here," Sophia whispered, motioning for her daughter to hide behind the overturned trunk.

She stepped outside, scanning the perimeter with the flashlight. The beam caught a fleeting glimpse of a figure disappearing into the trees.

"Who's there?" Sophia called out, but there was no response.

When she returned inside, she found Lily staring at the journal, tears streaming down her face.

"What's wrong, sweetheart?" Sophia asked, rushing to her.

Lily pointed to an entry she hadn't noticed before:

"If you find this, leave. You're not safe here. They know about the cabin."

Sophia's blood ran cold.

Fleeing the Cabin

Sophia didn't hesitate. "We need to go," she said, stuffing the journal and letters into her bag.

"What about the rest of the stuff?" Lily asked, her voice quivering.

"We can't stay," Sophia replied. "It's too dangerous."

They hurried to the car, Sophia's eyes darting between the shadows as they loaded their belongings. The sense of being watched was palpable, every rustle of leaves a potential threat.

As they drove away, Sophia couldn't shake the feeling that their ordeal was far from over. The cabin had provided more questions than answers, and whoever—or whatever—was after them wasn't giving up.

Chapter Eight: The Revelation

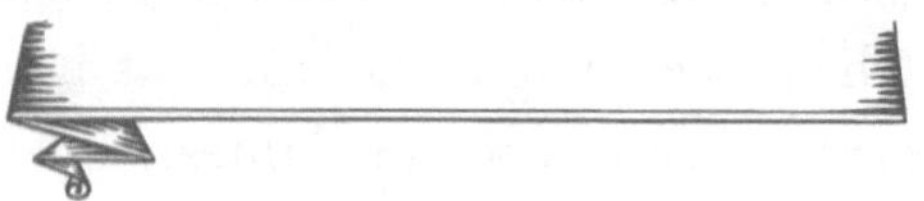

Section One: Unearthed Truths

Sophia gripped the steering wheel as the car sped away from the cabin, the silence inside the vehicle broken only by the occasional rustling of papers and the hum of the engine. Lily sat in the backseat, clutching the locket as if it were her lifeline.

"Mom," Lily whispered, her voice trembling.

Sophia glanced at her through the rearview mirror, her heart sinking at the sight of her daughter's pale face.

"What is it, honey?" Sophia asked.

"It's not over," Lily said, clutching the locket tighter. "I can feel it."

Sophia exhaled, trying to calm her racing thoughts. She didn't doubt her daughter anymore—not after the dreams, the sketches, the eerie knowledge that no child her age should possess.

As they reached the outskirts of town, Sophia pulled over at a secluded rest stop. She turned off the engine and faced Lily.

"We need to figure out our next move," she said, her voice steady but firm.

Lily opened the journal they had taken from the cabin, flipping to one of the final entries. The words seemed to leap off the page:

"There is no running from the truth. It's bigger than me, bigger than her. If you've found this, you need to know: the answers lie where it all began."

"Where it all began," Sophia murmured, her mind racing.

Section Two: Tracing the Beginning

Sophia spent hours poring over the journal and the letters in the parking lot. One of the letters contained a return address—a small town called Cedar Ridge, two hours away.

"That has to be it," Sophia said, showing the letter to Lily.

Lily nodded solemnly. "She wants us to go there."

The drive to Cedar Ridge was filled with an uneasy anticipation. The sun was beginning to set by the time they arrived, casting the town in an eerie twilight.

The return address led them to an old, abandoned library on the edge of town. Its windows were boarded up, and the sign above the door was barely legible.

"Are you sure about this?" Sophia asked, glancing at Lily.

Lily nodded. "This is where she wants us to be."

SECTION THREE: THE Hidden Room

The library's interior was dark and dusty, the air thick with the smell of mildew and forgotten history. Sophia used her flashlight to guide them through the maze of shelves.

Lily tugged on her sleeve, pointing to a trapdoor hidden beneath a threadbare rug.

"How did you know that was there?" Sophia asked, her voice tinged with awe.

"I just know," Lily replied simply.

Sophia hesitated for a moment before prying open the trapdoor. A narrow staircase descended into the darkness below.

The basement was unlike anything Sophia had expected. The walls were lined with photographs, newspaper clippings, and handwritten notes—all connected by a web of red string.

At the center of it all was a single word: **"Lily."**

Section Four: Confronting the Truth

Sophia's knees buckled, and she steadied herself against the wall.

"This can't be real," she whispered.

Lily approached the wall, her fingers tracing the lines of string. "She knew about me before I was even born," she said, her voice filled with a mix of fear and wonder.

Sophia's gaze fell on a stack of files on a nearby table. She opened one to find medical records, birth certificates, and adoption papers—all connected to Clara Bennett and her own family.

"This is impossible," Sophia said, her hands trembling as she sifted through the documents. "How could Clara know about you?"

A voice from the shadows answered her.

"Because she was trying to protect her."

Sophia spun around, her flashlight illuminating the figure of an older man stepping out from the darkness.

Section Five: The Guardian's Tale

The man introduced himself as Marcus Hensley, the son of Thomas Hensley, the cabin's original owner. He explained that Clara had come to him years ago, desperate for help.

"She was convinced that your daughter was the key to something she couldn't fully understand," Marcus said.

Sophia's mind raced. "But why? What does this have to do with Lily?"

Marcus hesitated before responding. "Because Lily isn't just a reincarnation. She's part of a cycle—a cycle that has been repeating for generations. And you're not the first mother to uncover it."

Section Six: The Connection to Clara

Marcus led them to a hidden room filled with artifacts—old journals, paintings, and relics that spanned centuries. Each item depicted a young girl who bore an uncanny resemblance to Lily.

"Clara believed that Lily was the next in line," Marcus said. "She thought that by uncovering the truth, she could break the cycle."

Sophia stared at the artifacts, her mind overwhelmed by the weight of the revelation. "What does this mean for Lily?" she asked.

Marcus's expression was grave. "It means she's in danger. There are people who would do anything to control her—or eliminate her."

Section Seven: A New Resolve

Sophia knew she couldn't allow anyone to harm her daughter. She resolved to continue Clara's work, to uncover the full truth and protect Lily at all costs.

As they left the library, Marcus handed Sophia a key. "This opens a safety deposit box in the next town. Inside, you'll find everything Clara left behind. Use it wisely."

Sophia thanked him and led Lily back to the car. The road ahead was uncertain, but one thing was clear: their journey was far from over.

Section Eight: The Safety Deposit Box

Sophia and Lily arrived in the neighboring town of Maplewood the following morning. The safety deposit box was located in a modest, brick-walled bank that seemed untouched by time.

Sophia approached the counter with the key Marcus had given her.

"I need access to this box," she said, her voice steady but tinged with urgency.

The teller inspected the key and nodded, leading them to a secure room in the back. When the box was opened, its contents revealed a collection of photographs, an old cassette tape, and a sealed envelope addressed to Sophia.

Sophia's hands trembled as she opened the envelope. The letter inside, written in Clara's handwriting, began:

"If you're reading this, it means the cycle has begun again. I'm sorry you had to be the one to carry this burden, but I believe you're strong enough to see it through."

The letter detailed Clara's findings about the cyclical pattern of girls like Lily, all possessing the same eerie traits and connections to events that defied logic. It also warned of an organization called *The Covenant*, a secretive group that sought to control the girls for their own gain.

Sophia's heart sank as she realized the enormity of what they were up against.

Section Nine: The Tape's Message

Back in their motel room, Sophia played the cassette tape. Clara's voice crackled through the speaker, filled with a mix of urgency and fear.

"I've uncovered something they don't want the world to know. These girls... they aren't just reincarnations. They're vessels for something ancient, something powerful. The Covenant will stop at nothing to harness that power. If you're hearing this, you need to protect Lily at all costs. They'll come for her, just like they came for me."

The tape ended abruptly, leaving Sophia and Lily in stunned silence.

"What do they want with me?" Lily asked, her voice barely above a whisper.

Sophia knelt beside her, holding her hands tightly. "They won't get to you. I promise."

Section Ten: A Shadowed Pursuit

That night, Sophia couldn't shake the feeling of being watched. She double-checked the motel's locks and kept a knife within reach.

Lily's restless dreams returned, and she murmured cryptic phrases in her sleep:

"The tower stands tall... the circle must break... she's waiting in the light."

Sophia jotted down every word, determined to piece together their meaning.

The next morning, as they prepared to leave, Sophia noticed a black SUV parked across the street. It had been there when they arrived, and its occupants seemed intent on remaining unnoticed.

"They're watching us," Sophia whispered, her instincts on high alert.

Without hesitation, she packed their belongings and led Lily to the car. They needed to stay ahead of *The Covenant*.

Section Eleven: The Tower's Clue

Sophia and Lily drove for hours, guided by the cryptic phrases from Lily's dreams. They stopped at a roadside diner to gather their thoughts.

"The tower," Sophia mused aloud, sketching a crude drawing on a napkin. "It has to mean something. Do you remember anything else from your dream?"

Lily closed her eyes, her small hands clutching the locket tightly. "There was a bell... and a name. 'Evergreen.'"

Sophia's eyes widened. Evergreen Tower was a long-abandoned lighthouse along the coast, notorious for its dark history and rumored hauntings.

"That's where we need to go," Sophia said, her resolve firm.

Section Twelve: The Lighthouse Revelation

Evergreen Tower loomed against the stormy sky, its once-pristine structure now weathered and crumbling.

Sophia and Lily climbed the winding staircase to the top, where they found a hidden compartment beneath the old bell. Inside was a journal, its pages yellowed with age.

The journal belonged to a woman named Margaret Hensley, a distant ancestor of Marcus. Her entries mirrored Clara's discoveries, describing a recurring pattern of girls like Lily and the ancient power they carried.

But the final entry was chilling:

"The Covenant will stop at nothing to claim the vessel. If they succeed, it will be the end of us all."

As Sophia read aloud, the wind howled through the cracks in the tower, and Lily clutched her mother's arm.

"What does it mean, Mom?" Lily asked, her voice trembling.

"It means we have to stop them," Sophia replied, her determination solidifying.

Section Thirteen: The Covenant Strikes

As they descended the tower, the sound of footsteps echoed from below. Sophia's heart raced as she realized they weren't alone.

"Run!" she whispered to Lily, pushing her toward a hidden exit.

The two made their way through the lighthouse's dark corridors, evading the men dressed in black who had surrounded the building.

Sophia's mind raced as she plotted their next move. They couldn't keep running forever.

Section Fourteen: A New Ally

Once they escaped, Sophia reached out to Marcus for help. He directed them to a safe house, where they were met by a woman named Evelyn, a former member of *The Covenant* who had defected years ago.

Evelyn provided crucial insight into the organization's plans and its connection to the cycle of reincarnations.

"They believe Lily is the key to unlocking an ancient power," Evelyn explained. "But they don't understand the consequences of their actions."

Sophia and Evelyn began devising a plan to take down *The Covenant* and protect Lily from their grasp.

Chapter Nine: Echoes of the Missing

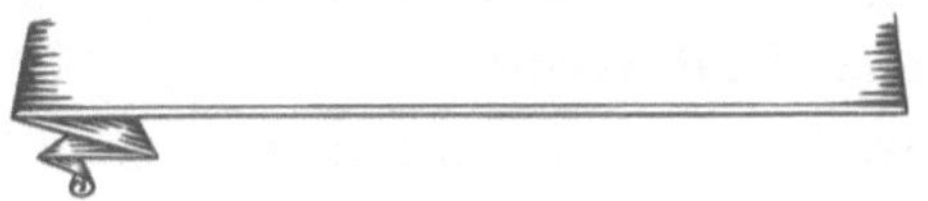

Section One: Into the Heart of the Mystery

Sophia's heart pounded as she and Evelyn prepared for the next phase of their journey. They were venturing into the stronghold of *The Covenant*, a sprawling estate hidden in the dense forest on the outskirts of Maplewood. Evelyn, armed with her knowledge as a former member, had mapped out a way inside.

Lily clung to her mother's hand, her eyes wide with apprehension. "What if they catch us?"

"They won't," Sophia said firmly, though her voice wavered. "We'll get in, find the answers we need, and get out."

Evelyn placed a hand on Sophia's shoulder. "We have to be ready for anything. They'll fight to keep their secrets buried."

The group approached the estate under the cover of night. The towering iron gates, adorned with arcane symbols, loomed ominously before them.

Section Two: The Hidden Archives

Inside the estate, the trio maneuvered through shadowed hallways, avoiding roving guards. Evelyn led them to a concealed door in the library, marked by a faint carving of an ancient sigil.

"This is it," Evelyn whispered, pressing a sequence of symbols that caused the door to creak open.

The room beyond was filled with books, scrolls, and artifacts that seemed to radiate an unsettling energy. At the center stood a pedestal with a glass case containing a weathered leather-bound journal.

Sophia opened the journal and began reading aloud. It chronicled centuries of experiments, rituals, and observations by *The Covenant*, all centered on individuals like Lily.

"They've been doing this for generations," Sophia said, her voice trembling. "Using these children as tools for their own gain."

Section Three: The Revelation

As they delved deeper into the journal, Sophia found entries detailing Clara Bennett's life and ultimate demise. Clara had been the first to uncover the cycle's true purpose: not just to harness power but to prevent an apocalyptic event.

One entry sent chills down Sophia's spine:

"The vessel must choose: to embrace their role as a guardian or let the cycle repeat, risking unimaginable consequences."

Evelyn's face paled as she explained. "Lily isn't just a target. She's the key to either breaking the cycle or perpetuating it."

Sophia turned to her daughter, who had been silently listening. "Lily, do you understand what this means?"

Lily nodded slowly. "I think so. It's why I've been dreaming... why I can see her memories."

Section Four: The Ritual Hall

The sound of footsteps interrupted their discovery. Guards poured into the room, forcing Sophia and Evelyn to grab Lily and flee. They raced through the estate, finally stumbling into a grand hall with towering pillars and intricate carvings depicting the cycle.

At the center of the room was a raised platform with an ancient artifact—a crystalline orb pulsating with light.

"That's it," Evelyn said, her voice barely audible. "That's the source of their power."

But before they could approach, they were surrounded. A man stepped forward, his presence commanding.

"Welcome," he said, his voice smooth yet menacing. "You've come far, but this is where your journey ends."

Section Five: A Battle for Control

The man, who introduced himself as Elias, leader of *The Covenant*, explained his intentions. He believed Lily was the perfect vessel to unlock the orb's full potential.

"She has the memories, the visions. She is destined for this," Elias said.

Sophia stepped forward, shielding Lily. "She's just a child. You can't force this on her."

"It's not forcing if it's destiny," Elias countered.

Sophia and Evelyn fought back with everything they had. Evelyn used her insider knowledge to sabotage the guards' weapons, while Sophia used her instincts and sheer determination to protect Lily.

Amid the chaos, Lily stood frozen, staring at the orb. Its light seemed to call to her, filling her with a mix of fear and longing.

Section Six: Lily's Choice

As the battle raged on, Lily approached the orb. Sophia screamed for her to stop, but Lily shook her head.

"I have to do this, Mom," she said, her voice steady despite her tears. "I have to end this."

Lily placed her hands on the orb, and the room filled with blinding light.

In that moment, Lily was transported to a liminal space, where she came face-to-face with Clara Bennett.

"Lily," Clara said gently, "you have the power to break the cycle. But it will come at a cost."

"What cost?" Lily asked, her voice trembling.

"You'll lose a part of yourself," Clara replied. "But you'll save countless others."

Section Seven: The Breaking of the Cycle

Back in the hall, the light from the orb intensified, knocking everyone to the ground. Sophia crawled toward Lily, shielding her eyes from the brilliance.

Lily screamed as the orb shattered, sending waves of energy through the estate.

The carvings on the walls began to crumble, and the ancient power *The Covenant* had relied on for centuries dissipated.

Elias and his followers fled, their plans in ruins. Evelyn helped Sophia carry Lily out of the estate as the structure began to collapse.

Section Eight: Aftermath

Days later, Sophia and Lily returned home. Lily was quieter, her vibrant personality dimmed by the ordeal.

Sophia knew that her daughter had sacrificed something profound to end the cycle, but she also knew it was the only way to ensure their safety.

Evelyn stayed with them for a while, helping them adjust and ensuring *The Covenant* wouldn't resurface.

Sophia began writing Clara's story, determined to honor her sacrifice and ensure the truth was never forgotten.

Section Nine: The Price of Sacrifice

In the days that followed, Sophia noticed subtle changes in Lily. She was quieter, more introspective, and often seemed lost in thought. The brightness in her eyes had dimmed, replaced by a solemnity that Sophia couldn't ignore.

One night, as Sophia tucked her daughter into bed, she asked gently, "Lily, are you okay?"

Lily hesitated, her small hands clutching the edge of her blanket. "I feel... different, Mom. Like a part of me is missing."

Sophia's heart broke as she realized the depth of Lily's sacrifice. The connection to Clara, the dreams, the memories—everything that had linked Lily to the past—was gone, leaving an emptiness that words couldn't fill.

"You're so brave," Sophia whispered, brushing a strand of hair from Lily's face. "And I'm so proud of you."

Section Ten: A New Chapter

With *The Covenant* dismantled and their power broken, the town of Maplewood began to heal. Rumors of the estate's collapse spread, but the true story remained a closely guarded secret.

Evelyn worked tirelessly to ensure that any remnants of *The Covenant's* influence were destroyed. She burned the journals, smashed the artifacts, and erased every trace of the group's existence.

"This is for Lily," Evelyn said as she destroyed the last of the documents. "So she can grow up without this shadow hanging over her."

Sophia, meanwhile, focused on rebuilding her family's life. She enrolled Lily in art therapy, hoping it would help her process her experiences. The sessions brought glimpses of the old Lily—moments of laughter, flashes of creativity—but it was clear the journey to healing would be long.

Section Eleven: Clara's Legacy

One evening, as Sophia sorted through the few items they had salvaged from the estate, she came across a small locket with Clara's initials engraved on the back. Inside was a faded photograph of Clara as a young girl, smiling brightly.

Sophia felt a pang of connection, as if Clara's spirit lingered, watching over them.

She decided to write a book about Clara's life, the mysterious cycle, and the courage it took to break it. The process was both cathartic and painful, forcing Sophia to confront the horrors they had faced.

Lily often sat beside her as she wrote, drawing pictures inspired by their journey. One of her sketches depicted Clara standing beside Lily, both smiling—a poignant reminder of the bond they had shared across time.

Section Twelve: Shadows of the Future

Though the immediate danger had passed, Sophia couldn't shake the feeling that their story wasn't entirely over. She often found herself glancing over her shoulder, wary of unseen threats.

Evelyn reassured her. "*The Covenant* is gone. You and Lily are safe."

But Sophia knew better than to be complacent. She began taking self-defense classes and installed state-of-the-art security systems in their home.

Her paranoia wasn't entirely unfounded. Strange letters began arriving in the mail—cryptic messages written in an ancient script. Evelyn identified them as warnings, left by rogue members of *The Covenant* who still clung to their shattered beliefs.

"They're fractured, scattered," Evelyn said. "But they're watching."

SECTION THIRTEEN: THE Power Within

Despite the lingering unease, Lily began to find her own strength. Her dreams, though no longer supernatural, returned in vivid detail. She often shared them with Sophia, who marveled at her daughter's resilience.

"Maybe it's a gift," Lily said one day. "Maybe I'm supposed to use what I've learned to help others."

Sophia felt a swell of pride. "You've always had a gift, Lily. You're stronger than you know."

Inspired by her daughter's bravery, Sophia decided to expand her writing into advocacy. She partnered with Evelyn to create a foundation dedicated to protecting children who might be exploited by dangerous groups like *The Covenant*.

Section Fourteen: A Faint Echo

Years later, as Lily prepared to leave for college, she stumbled upon the locket again. She held it up to the light, studying Clara's face.

"I think she's at peace now," Lily said softly.

Sophia nodded. "And so are we."

Though the memories of their ordeal had faded with time, the lessons remained. Lily had grown into a compassionate, determined young woman, shaped by the trials she had endured but not defined by them.

As they stood together, watching the sunset from their porch, a faint breeze rustled the trees. It carried with it a whisper—soft, almost imperceptible, but unmistakably Clara's voice.

"Thank you."

Chapter Ten: Shadows of Resolution

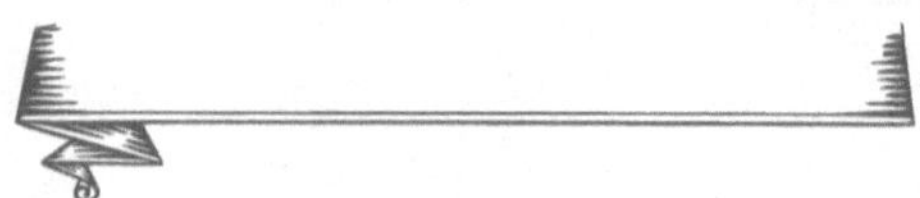

Sophia sat at the edge of her bed, staring at the flickering light of a single candle on her nightstand. The flame danced and twisted, casting elongated shadows across the room. These shadows felt like reflections of her thoughts—unpredictable, chaotic, and consuming. The ordeal she and Lily had endured had left scars, and though the immediate danger seemed to have passed, the questions and unresolved fears loomed over her like a storm cloud.

This was no longer just about survival. It was about ensuring safety for Lily and finding peace for herself. To do that, she had to confront the question she had been avoiding: how far was she willing to go to uncover the truth and protect her family?

Section One: A Whisper in the Dark

In the quiet moments before dawn, Sophia began gathering everything she had learned. She laid out photos, notes, and fragments of old documents on her dining table, creating a mosaic of the tangled web she had unraveled.

Evelyn joined her, holding two steaming mugs of coffee. "It's not healthy to keep revisiting this," Evelyn said gently.

Sophia shook her head. "If we don't face it now, it will always be lurking in the shadows. I can't let this cycle of silence continue. We owe it to Clara, to Lily, to ourselves."

Evelyn sighed, setting the coffee down. "Then we need a plan. What's our next move?"

Sophia's answer came without hesitation. "We expose the truth."

Section Two: Allies and Enemies

Sophia knew she couldn't do this alone. She reached out to trusted individuals who had connections to law enforcement, journalism, and academia. Among them was Detective Marcus Hale, who had been investigating Clara Bennett's disappearance years before but had been forced to abandon the case due to political pressure.

"I never believed the official story," Marcus admitted during their first meeting. "Clara's disappearance was too clean, too convenient for those in power."

Sophia shared her findings, and as Marcus pored over the evidence, his determination reignited. "This could blow the case wide open. But you need to be prepared. Once you go public, there's no turning back."

Sophia nodded. "I understand the risks. But I won't let fear silence me anymore."

SECTION THREE: THE Web Tightens

As Sophia's investigation gained momentum, threats began to surface. Unmarked envelopes containing cryptic warnings appeared in her mailbox. A car followed her late at night. The sense of being watched became a constant, suffocating presence.

Evelyn grew increasingly concerned. "Sophia, we need to pull back. These people—whoever they are—won't hesitate to hurt us."

But Sophia was resolute. "If we stop now, they win. And they'll keep doing this to others."

The tension reached a breaking point when a brick was thrown through Sophia's window, a note attached with a single word: *STOP.*

Marcus increased patrols around Sophia's house and installed additional security measures. "We're not letting them intimidate us," he assured her.

Section Four: The Revelation

A breakthrough came when Marcus uncovered a forgotten safe deposit box registered under Clara Bennett's name. Inside, they found a diary filled with detailed accounts of her fears and suspicions in the days leading up to her disappearance.

"She knew she was in danger," Sophia whispered as she read Clara's words. "She tried to warn people, but no one listened."

The diary also included a list of names—key members of *The Covenant*—and a map marking the location of a hidden archive.

"This is it," Marcus said. "This is the smoking gun we've been looking for."

Section Five: Into the Lion's Den

The archive was located in an abandoned warehouse on the outskirts of town. Sophia, Marcus, and Evelyn decided to retrieve the evidence themselves, knowing that involving too many people could jeopardize the mission.

The night they chose was cold and silent. Armed with flashlights and determination, they navigated the crumbling structure until they found a locked room hidden behind a false wall.

Inside were stacks of documents, videotapes, and artifacts—irrefutable evidence of *The Covenant's* activities. Among them was a chilling video of Clara being interrogated, her voice defiant despite the fear in her eyes.

Sophia clenched her fists. "They took everything from her. We can't let them get away with this."

Section Six: The Price of Truth

Releasing the evidence to the public was not without consequences. News outlets exploded with coverage, and the names of *The Covenant's* members were exposed. Protests erupted, demanding justice for Clara and others who had been victimized.

But *The Covenant* fought back. They hired high-profile lawyers, discredited witnesses, and manipulated the narrative to paint themselves as victims of a smear campaign.

Sophia found herself at the center of a media frenzy. Reporters camped outside her house, and online trolls bombarded her with threats.

Evelyn stood by her side. "You've done the right thing, Sophia. Don't let them break you."

Section Seven: A Glimmer of Hope

Despite the chaos, there were moments of triumph. Survivors of *The Covenant* began coming forward, emboldened by Sophia's bravery.

"I thought no one would ever believe me," one woman tearfully admitted during an interview.

Lily, too, found her voice. During a televised press conference, she shared her experiences with the dreams and how they had led to the truth.

"I was scared," Lily said. "But my mom taught me that doing the right thing is worth the risk."

The room erupted in applause, and Sophia felt a surge of pride.

Section Eight: Shadows of Resolution

As the legal battles unfolded, Sophia reflected on the journey that had brought her here. She had faced unimaginable horrors, but she had also discovered her own strength.

One evening, as she and Lily sat together watching the sunset, Sophia said, "I hope you know how brave you are."

Lily smiled. "I learned from the best."

Though the fight against *The Covenant* was far from over, Sophia knew they had already won a significant victory. They had broken the cycle of silence and fear, ensuring that Clara's story—and her own—would never be forgotten.

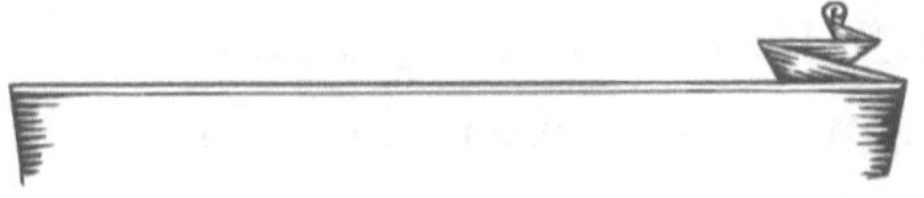

Epilogue: Lingering Whispers

The sun dipped below the horizon, casting a soft golden light across the landscape. The world seemed peaceful, as though the chaos of the past had faded into the quiet, distant past. Yet, for Sophia Reed, peace was a concept that felt both foreign and unattainable.

As she stood at the edge of her porch, watching Lily play in the yard, a pang of bitter sweetness tugged at her heart. The battle for truth, the fight to uncover Clara Bennett's hidden past, and the journey to protect her daughter had changed them in ways that words could scarcely express. The scars they bore weren't just physical—they were etched deeply into their souls.

Sophia turned her gaze to the sky, feeling the weight of the world pressing down on her. The echoes of the missing, of Clara Bennett, and of *The Covenant* still reverberated in her mind, a constant reminder of the price she had paid for answers.

The past was never truly gone. The threads of her investigation, the connections she had uncovered, still lingered, quietly whispering in the corners of her consciousness. Even though the public was now aware of the truth, the repercussions of what had been exposed were far from over. *The Covenant* had been disbanded, its members disgraced or imprisoned, but the ripples of their actions stretched further than Sophia could have ever imagined. There were more stories to be told, more lives to be rebuilt.

A DISTANT MEMORY, A Lasting Legacy

Sophia thought of Clara often. The woman whose disappearance had ignited this chain of events. The woman whose life had been a mystery, but whose bravery had given Sophia the strength to continue. Clara's sacrifice had not been in vain, but it had come at a tremendous cost.

The investigation into Clara's past was now public knowledge, her diaries, video recordings, and the shocking truth about *The Covenant* forever etched into history. The truth, however, was only part of the equation. There was something more profound—something that could never be fully understood or explained. Clara's story was now a part of their family's story, and in that, Sophia found both a sense of closure and an aching emptiness.

Clara had been more than a victim. She had been a beacon, a lighthouse shining through the storm. Sophia's only hope now was that Lily could one day understand the full scope of what had transpired—the depth of the courage it took to face the truth and the sacrifices that were made for it.

The Price of Answers

Answers, Sophia had learned, often came with a steep price. The truth they had unearthed had shaken the foundations of her life and the lives of those around her. The people she had once trusted, the friends she had known, had turned out to be something else entirely. The realization that nothing and no one was quite as they seemed left Sophia with a profound sense of isolation.

There were moments when she wondered if the cost had been too high. In the pursuit of justice, she had risked everything—her peace, her sense of safety, her relationships, and even her own identity. Yet, there was no going back. The echoes of the past had shaped her, and the truth she had fought for had not only changed the world but had also transformed her as a person.

The world would never be the same again. The past was not something that could be erased, but it could be faced, acknowledged, and used to build a better future. Sophia had come to understand that the quest for truth was both a burden and a gift.

Echoes That Remain

As time passed, the whispers of the past didn't fade. They lingered like the faintest sound, always there, just out of reach. For some, they were a reminder of what had been lost, of lives stolen, and of justice delayed. For others, they were a call to remember—never forget, never stop searching.

Sophia had often wondered what life would have been like had Clara's disappearance never occurred. Would she have lived her life in oblivion, unaware of the dangerous secrets that lurked beneath the surface of their town? Would she have been content, ignorant of the dark forces at play? But deep down, she knew that she would never have been able to live with that ignorance. Some truths were meant to be discovered, even at great personal cost.

Lily was growing up. Though she would never fully comprehend the events of the past, Sophia could see the influence of everything they had been through in the way she viewed the world. Lily had inherited her mother's courage and resilience. She was a child of the truth, of secrets revealed, and of justice fought for.

One evening, as they sat together on the couch, Lily rested her head on Sophia's shoulder. "Do you think we'll ever be free of it all?" she asked quietly.

Sophia's hand gently stroked Lily's hair, her heart heavy with the weight of the question. "I don't know," she replied softly. "But we're stronger now, and we'll keep moving forward. We'll always remember what happened, but we'll also keep living. The world may try to forget, but we won't."

Sophia smiled faintly as Lily drifted off to sleep, the past still lingering but no longer controlling them. For the first time in a long while, Sophia allowed herself to believe that they could find a semblance of peace. The journey had been long and painful, but it had brought them here—together, in the quiet after the storm. And though the shadows of the missing would always be with them, they no longer cast a shadow over their lives.

The echoes remained, but so did their strength. And that was enough.

The End

Don't miss out!

Visit the website below and you can sign up to receive emails whenever Cindy C publishes a new book. There's no charge and no obligation.

https://books2read.com/r/B-A-ZJIWB-YVJMF

BOOKS 2 READ

Connecting independent readers to independent writers.